alien

KID 2

Goshen`s Secret

alien KID 2

Goshen's Secret

Kristen Otte

ISBN-10: 1975840011
ISBN-13: 978-1975840013

This book is dedicated to the kids who feel like aliens in their school. Hang in there.

One

As Mrs. Felder approached my desk, I couldn't stop staring at her belly.

Is she hiding a basketball under her dress? No way, that can't be it. I looked again at her gigantic, round stomach. *That can't be healthy.*

"Charlie, this wasn't your best work," she said. Her stomach grazed my shoulder as she placed my paper on the desk. A "B-" was written across the top in blue pen with a few sentences on the bottom of the paper detailing why. I put the paper in my folder and watched Mrs. Felder waddle to the front of the room.

"In case you haven't heard, today is my last day before I go on maternity leave. I plan on returning in January. Until then, you are expected to do your best work for Mr. Goshen."

"Maternity leave?" I whispered to nobody in particular. "What is she talking about?"

"Charlie, do you have a question?" I looked around the room. None of my classmates looked confused or alarmed about Mrs. Felder leaving. Clearly, I was missing something important. *Should I read her mind?* My parents didn't like me using my alien ability because I hadn't completed my training yet.

"No," I said. The bell rang. I stood from my desk and filed out of the classroom with my classmates to my locker.

"Maya, I have a dumb question," I asked at our lockers. Maya had the locker next to mine and had become my first friend in Silver Lake. She knew I was an alien.

"Oh, no," she said. I sneered. "What is it?"

"Mrs. Felder announced she was leaving for maternity. What is that?"

"You don't know what that means?"

I shook my head.

"Haven't you noticed her belly?"

"How can you not notice it?"

"She's pregnant, Charlie."

"Pregnant?"

"Do aliens on your planet not get pregnant?"

"Europa is one of Jupiter's moons."

"Whatever."

"Pregnant?" I asked again.

"She is going to have a baby."

"That belly is a baby?"

"Yes."

"Hot diggity dog!"

"What did you say?"

I grinned. "It's one of my new sayings. I'm trying it out. What do you think?"

"Oh, Charlie." She smiled. "We better get to class."

Maya and I shut our lockers and went to history, our last class of the day. She sat in the seat behind me. I turned around.

"Were you serious about the baby?" I asked.

The bell rang. "Quiet down class," Mrs. Roberts said. "We have a lot to cover today." I looked at Maya's grin. She wasn't going to tell me the answer.

I sighed and turned around to face the front of the room. Maya and I had a deal that I wasn't allowed to read her mind at all. I'd have to find out about the Mrs. Felder having a baby on my own.

It felt like history class took four hours, not forty minutes. History was my least favorite class because most of the time we had to read the textbook and then fill in a handout. The worst part was that I wanted to know more about the history of America because it would help me understand my life here on Earth. *But why does it have to be so boring?* There had to be a better way to learn this stuff.

When class ended, I turned to Maya.

"You're not going to tell me, are you?" I asked.

"Charlie, here's what I know. Mrs. Felder is going to have a baby very soon. That's why her belly is so big."

"Wow."

"Then she will stay home with the baby for a few months. It's normal for a mom to stay home with a baby for a couple months. That's called maternity leave."

"That's why Mrs. Felder won't be back until January," I said.

"If you didn't know Mrs. Felder was pregnant, what did you think was happening to her?"

"I thought she might have a basketball in her dress."

"What?"

"That's what it looks like!"

Maya laughed. "You seriously thought that?"

"It was more of a funny idea. Really, I thought she needed to take a break from the carrots."

"Carrots?"

"Yes. Whenever I see her at lunch, she's eating carrots."

Maya shook her head. "Carrots won't make her fat."

"Why not?"

"Because they are good for you."

"Even if you ate a thousand carrots in a day?"

"Who eats a thousand carrots in a day?"

"Maybe Mrs. Felder!"

"Charlie, you are a lost cause."

"I thought I was getting the hang of this middle-school thing."

"You have so much to learn."

"Maybe, but I'm getting closer."

"Closer to what?"

"Closer to … I don't know."

We opened the doors and walked outside into the cool air. The skies were overcast, and a crisp breeze rippled through my hair.

"I like Mrs. Felder. She is a good teacher. Do you know anything about who is filling in for her?" I asked.

"I don't know anything about the sub."

"Sub? Why are you talking about an underwater boat?"

"No, sub can mean a substitute teacher."

"Lickity split. You're right. I am a lost cause."

We smiled and went to the next class.

When I entered English class on Monday, our substitute teacher was not what I was expecting. He was a monster of a man, standing at least six feet tall, with biceps muscles bursting through his green polo shirt. His brown hair was buzz cut, and he had a goatee. When he smiled, I swear his perfectly white teeth sparkled.

"I am Mr. Goshen. I will be your English teacher until Mrs. Felder returns," he said with a high-pitched voice that reminded me of Mickey Mouse. A few boys in the class giggled. He stared at them and shook his head no.

"I want to cover a few ground rules before we get started. Don't expect that this will be an easy class with Mrs. Felder gone. You still need to work hard. I expect the best from all of you, and I will not tolerate any disrespect. Any questions?" He surveyed the room. "Let's get started. I read through the latest assignments that you completed for Mrs. Felder. It is clear that most of the class doesn't understand basic grammar rules. That's where we will start."

A few students in the room groaned. The smile on his face turned to a frown, and he glared at the room. The moment passed, and he grabbed a stack of papers from his desk.

"Alicia, will you hand these out?" Alicia smiled and passed out the handouts to the entire class before returning to her seat.

We worked through the grammar handout as a class. Mr. Goshen called on students at random for answers, unlike Mrs. Felder, who only called on volunteers. As the questions increased in difficulty, more students answered the questions incorrectly. When it was my turn to answer the question, I tried to read Mr. Goshen's mind. He was on the other side of the classroom, so I couldn't separate his thoughts from all the students around me. Reading minds becomes more difficult with more people around. I looked at the sentence and guessed. Somehow I got the answer right.

"Great work, Charlie. If only the rest of the class was as bright as you," he said. I didn't respond. It seemed like a trap, and I didn't want my classmates mad at me.

"Suck-up," someone muttered. I couldn't tell who said it.

"Speak up," Mr. Goshen bellowed. He walked down the aisle next to Jordan's desk.

"What did you say, Jordan?" Jordan didn't flinch. Mr. Goshen marched back to his desk, scribbled something on a pink piece of paper, and then returned to Jordan's desk. He handed the slip to Jordan. "Go see Principal Stevens."

"Are you serious? I didn't do anything."

"You were being disrespectful to another student," Mr. Goshen said. "That's not acceptable."

Jordan grabbed his things and left the room; the door slammed behind him. I sat facing forward, but my mind drifted a bit, and I read the minds of a few nearby students. They were worried and a little bit anxious. I tuned out of their heads and looked at the clock. We only had a few minutes left.

Mr. Goshen passed out three double-sided handouts to complete for homework. The room remained eerily quiet until the bell rang.

After class, Maya was waiting for me at my locker.

"Did you hear what happened with Jordan?" I asked.

"No, why? Did something happen with you two?"

"No. Yes. Kind of. He called me a suck up, and Mr. Goshen sent him to the principal's office."

"Wait a second, Mr. Goshen sent him to the principal's office for that?"

"Yes. He called me a suck-up."

"Oh no," she said.

"What?"

"I don't think Caden and Jordan will ignore you anymore."

At the start of school last month, Caden and Jordan had decided to pick on me because I was the new kid. Maya and I teamed up to beat them in a game of dodgeball, and they hadn't bothered me since.

"Lickity split. I didn't do anything. That was all Mr. Goshen."

"I know, he sent Kylie to the office during my class."

"For what?"

"She complained about the grammar work."

My eyes widened. "That's it?" I asked.

"Well, she had a bad attitude toward him."

"Oh," I said.

"It's been one day, and I already want Mrs. Felder back. It's going to be a long three months without her," Maya said.

Two

When I walked into English class on Friday, the white board was filled with various punctuation marks. The bell rang, and Mr. Goshen walked out from behind his desk and began another day of grammar lessons. The lesson on punctuation ended with five minutes left in class. I thought we might catch a break from the homework since it was the weekend, but I was wrong. He passed out a handout with an assignment to read a book and answer the questions.

Lickity split! We have to read a whole book this weekend! I raised my hand.

"What is it?" Mr. Goshen said.

"What if you don't have the assigned book, *The Giver*?"

"Then I suggest you get it. It was on the list at the start of the school year."

"What list?"

"I'm not answering that question."

"But—"

"Charlie, enough from you. If you need the book, check it out from the library or buy a copy."

"But you said we have to read the book, not check it out." A few students chuckled.

"Silence!" He stared across the room, and the chatter and laughter faded. He looked at me. A chill went through me.

"One more smart word out of you and you will spend the rest of the day in the office."

"Who's office?" I asked.

"That's it." Mr. Goshen stomped over to his desk and wrote something. He marched over to me, handed me the pink slip, and motioned me to the door.

Oh booger. What did I just do? I looked at the slip.

"Where do I go?"

Mr. Goshen glared at me. I bit my lip.

"Go to the principal's office. I assume you know where it is."

"Yes." I stared at him.

"Go!" he said. I grabbed my books and hurried out of the room. There was a check mark next to discipline with "talking back to the teacher" written in the notes section. That sounded right. I was talking back and forth with Mr. Goshen, but I didn't understand why that meant I had to see the principal.

When I reached the office, I recognized the lady with glasses and dark, shoulder-length hair who sat at the front desk. Her name card read MRS. TURNER. I'd met her during my last trip to the office when I'd fallen asleep in class.

"Hi, Mrs. Turner," I smiled and handed her the slip.

"Take a seat. Principal Stevens will call you back when he's ready." She ducked into his office and returned a minute later. I slumped in the chair and watched the clock. The second hand had circled around six times when Principal Stevens called for me. I rose and walked into his office and sat across from him.

"Mr. Goshen says you were talking back. That is not acceptable behavior. Students shouldn't talk back to their teachers."

"I don't understand," I said. "I asked a few questions about the homework assignment. Is that talking back?"

"Clearly you did more than that."

"I didn't, I swear."

"Listen Charlie, this is your first trip to my office."

"Actually, it's my second. Mrs. Felder sent me here for falling asleep a few weeks ago." Mr. Stevens opened his mouth to speak but then shut it without saying a word. I focused on his mind to know if I was really in trouble.

Something is off about this kid. I need to keep my eye on him, he thought.

Why did Principal Stevens want his eye on me? How could he put his eye on me? That was a strange thing to say.

"I'll let you off with a warning this time, but if I hear that you are talking back with other teachers, then there will be consequences."

"Okay," I said, but I was still confused.

"You are dismissed."

I left the room, and Mrs. Turner wrote me a pass to history class. I walked back to class trying to make sense of everything that happened. I can't talk with teachers, and the principal wants to remove his eye. None of this made sense. *Oh booger, I need Maya!* At least I got out of half of history class.

When I arrived, Mrs. Roberts took the pink slip and gave me the day's handout. When I sat down, I felt a tap on my shoulder. I turned around.

"Where were you?" Maya whispered.

"Principal's office."

"Why?"

"Charlie, Maya, quiet. This is solo work time." I turned and faced the front. I didn't want to go back to the principal's office. I opened my history book and started on the work for the day. I felt a tap on my shoulder a few minutes later.

"Was it Mr. Goshen?" Maya asked.

"Yes. I'll tell you after school." I looked toward the front of the room. Mrs. Roberts was watching me. I gave her a small smile and went back to work. When the class ended, Maya and I walked to our lockers.

"So ..." Maya began.

"I have no idea what happened, Maya. I was asking Mr. Goshen about the paper and how to get the book, then I was sent to the office."

"Start at the beginning, word for word," she said. I told the entire story to her.

"Charlie, you need to be more careful about what you ask the teachers."

"What did I say?"

"Mr. Goshen thought you were talking back."

"What does that mean?"

"Giving him a bad attitude."

"Lickity split! I was asking a question."

"The questions you asked are common sense for us."

"Oh, booger."

"Charlie, did you know you can borrow books from the library? They will loan you books for a few weeks that you can take home. You bring it back when you are done."

"Hot Spaghetti! I didn't know that! No wonder he was mad. The meeting with the principal makes sense now."

"You only got a warning, right?" Maya asked.

"Yes. But I read his mind. He wants to keep his eye on me. How can he do that?"

"Don't get sent to the Principal's office, and you'll be fine."

"What about the eye?" I asked.

"What eye?"

"Principal Steven's eye."

"Oh!" Maya started laughing. When she caught her breath, she continued. "*Keep his eye on you* is a saying. It means to watch you to make sure you don't get in trouble again."

"He can't remove his eye and put it on me?"

"No."

"Oh, thank goodness!"

Maya chuckled again, and we started down the hallway to the gym.

"Charlie, slow down," she said. We were in the English wing, and Mr. Goshen's classroom was a few steps ahead.

"What?" I asked. I didn't see anyone, so I couldn't mind read.

"I hear voices." She took a few steps forward and stopped in front of the door, staying out of sight from anyone in the classroom. She pointed to her ear. I didn't have the best hearing, but I could make out Mr. Goshen's voice and … was that Caden?

Maya's eyes widened. I focused on her, but then I stopped myself. I couldn't break our rule. I wasn't supposed to read her mind.

"Charlie, let's go." She motioned me forward, and we hurried past the doorway and to the gym.

When we exited the school, I couldn't wait anymore.

"What happened? I couldn't hear."

"Caden and Mr. Goshen know each other somehow. They were talking about going to a wrestling match or something like that." Our pace sped up, which meant Maya was excited by this news.

"Wrestling? What's that?"

"The sport where two guys roll around on the ground and try to pin each other."

"Nothing you just said made sense. I have a funny picture in my head."

"It's probably right. Look it up later."

"Okay, but I don't get why you're so excited about this."

"I'm not excited."

"Maya, we are practically jogging home right now."

She looked at me and stopped. "I heard something else. Mr. Goshen told Caden not to worry about his English grade."

"So?"

"That means that Mr. Goshen isn't being fair."

"So? Is he really that bad? He's only been here for the week," I said.

"Charlie, you were sent to the principal's office. We have to read a book and do an assignment over the weekend. This isn't right for sixth grade!"

"Right."

"You think I'm crazy."

"No. I'm with you, but I don't know what we can do."

"We need to pay attention to Caden and Mr. Goshen. You can use your ability, and maybe it can help us."

"Okay, but what are we trying to do?" I asked.

"Get Mr. Goshen in trouble."

"Oh," I said, even if I wasn't sure about her idea. But I'd follow Maya's lead.

We were at the intersection where we split for our separate houses. "Before you go, how do you check out a book from the library?"

"You need a library card, so bring your mom or dad with you."

"That's it?"

"It's easy. You'll be fine," Maya said.

Three

"Hey, Mom," I said, entering our house.

"How was school?"

"I got sent to the principal's office today."

"Why were you in trouble?"

"I talked back to the teacher, but I didn't mean to."

My mom entered my head, searched the memories, and told me it would be fine. Communicating with my own family and race was so much easier than talking with humans. No guessing, only answers.

"Can you come to the library with me? I need to check out a book."

"Why do I need to be there?"

"I'm not sure, but Maya said you need to come."

"Okay, then."

My mom drove us to the library. We entered the doors, and I approached the first desk in the library. A younger lady with dark curly hair and glasses sat at the desk.

"I need to check out a book," I said.

"What book?"

"*The Giver* by Lois Lowry."

The lady typed something in the keyboard and then nodded. "You need to go to the young adult fiction section in the back. The books are organized alphabetically by author last name."

"That's it?"

"Yes, we have two copies of the book on the shelf for you to check out."

"Okay. Thanks."

I motioned to my mom. She followed me to the back of the library. Maya had recommended that I read Harry Potter, so since school started I had been coming to this section of the library and reading. But I had never taken a book from the library. I scanned the shelves and found *The Giver*. I took it off the shelf.

"That's it?" My mom asked.

"I guess so." We turned and walked back to the front of the library and out the doors with the book in hand.

A siren went off. My mom and I dropped to the floor on our stomachs. The book hit the ground next to me.

"What is going on?" I asked my mom from my position lying on the floor.

"I don't know," she whispered. I looked around to see the woman from the desk approaching us. A few people in the library were pointing and laughing at us.

"Lickity split," I said.

"What?"

"I think we did something stupid." I started to rise from the ground. My mother followed me, and the nice lady from the library desk approached us.

"I don't think you checked the book out correctly. Have you checked out a book before?" she asked.

"No," my mom and I said in unison.

"Follow me." She led us to a series of computers below a sign that said CHECK OUT.

"Oh, booger," I said.

"Excuse me?" she said.

"Don't mind him," my mom said. "He likes to say weird things."

"Hey!" I mumbled.

"Can I have your library card?" she asked.

"Which card is that?" my mother asked, looking through her wallet.

"It's a blue card with the name Silver Lake Library on it." The woman looked at the cards in my mom's wallet.

"I don't think I have one," my mom responded.

"Have you been here before?"

"No, I have not," my mom said. Her face was turning blue, and I could feel the embarrassment rising in her.

"We are new to Silver Lake," I said. "We are still learning the strings."

"Learning the ropes," my mom said.

The lady squinted at us. "Come back to the desk. I'll get you signed up."

We followed her. My mom filled out some paperwork and received three blue cards. We returned to the check-out station. She walked us through scanning the card and the book.

"You are all set," she said.

"Thank you," my mother said. We crossed through the doors, but no siren this time.

"That was interesting."

"Why do they have a siren for not checking out a book? That seems a bit extreme," I said.

"They are really serious about reading. I wonder what happens if you don't return a book."

"Probably jail," I said.

"You better return this book on time," she said. "Or maybe not. It could be a good experiment to see what happens." She chuckled.

"No thanks!" We drove home laughing about our adventure at the library.

I was a little shaky the rest of Friday evening. I kept hearing the siren in my head, so by Saturday morning I was ready to get out of the house. When I stepped outside, the skies were clear, but it was chilly. The season was changing, and over the next month the temperature would continue to drop. The sensation of feeling cold was strange because it wasn't something my natural body had ever felt on Europa. My parents told me it would be even colder in Silver Lake than in Cleveland. We'd spent our first six months on Earth in Cleveland before moving to Silver Lake last summer. On Europa the weather was terribly frigid at times, so I didn't want to think about the upcoming winter here.

Even with the chilly air, I wanted to go play basketball. I missed the guys, especially Blake. He had become a good friend since I started playing at the park after school. I hadn't played all week because of homework and bad weather, so I decided to go after I finished the English assignment.

I buckled down and started working. I read the book in one sitting and then flew through the questions, answering them as quickly as I could. I knew I could do better work, but I had basketball to play!

I finished the assignment just before lunch. In an attempt to eat what other Earthly families ate, my mother was fixing chicken nuggets and macaroni and cheese. Food on Earth was weird. The chicken nuggets were shaped like dinosaurs, but dinosaurs weren't real animals, so why make a chicken version of them?

The macaroni and cheese was equally confusing. The noodles were shaped like baseballs, footballs, and basketballs, but humans never ate those things. It made no sense, but since my mom was making it, I ate the dinosaurs and footballs.

When I finished, I changed into shorts and a hoodie. I grabbed my copy of *The Giver* to return to the library and threw it in my backpack along with a snack and a water bottle. Then I started the long walk to the park. The cool, light breeze put a chill in my body, but after a few minutes, I didn't feel cold anymore.

Blake, Malik, and a few more of the regular guys were at the park when I arrived.

"Hey, Charlie," Blake said. He passed me the ball. "We've missed you this week."

"School work."

"Yeah, I understand, but you can't miss time to play, especially with tryouts coming up at the end of the month."

"Tryouts?" I asked. "What do you mean?"

"Aren't you going to try out for the basketball team at Silver Lake?"

"Oh, booger, I don't know."

"Did you say something about boogers?" Malik asked through a giggle.

"I thought that's why you started coming," Blake said.

"Nope. I just wanted to learn an Earthly game."

"A what?"

Lickity split.

"I wanted to learn how to play basketball. It seemed like fun," I said, trying to cover my slipup.

"You've gotten pretty good. You should try out," Blake said, ignoring my Earth comment. *That was a close one.*

"How do I try out?"

"They will announce when sixth-grade basketball tryouts are being held. Show up, follow the directions, and play your best."

"Will you be there?"

"No. I go to a different school, remember."

"Right."

"Did you have sports at your old school?"

"No."

"Makes sense."

"You really think I could make the team?" I knew that sports teams were a thing in middle school, but after my missteps in gym class, playing on any sports ball team seemed like an unreachable goal.

"You're short, but that shouldn't matter too much in middle school. If you can keep up with us, you can keep up with anyone."

"Even Caden?"

"Definitely."

"Hot Spaghetti!" I said.

Blake cracked up with laughter. "You say the weirdest things."

"I think everyone says weird things on Earth." *Lickity split. I did it again. I'm too comfortable with them.* I looked at Blake and focused on his thoughts. He was thinking about me being a little weird, but no thoughts about me being an alien.

"Are we waiting for anyone?" I said, changing the subject from my weirdness.

"Nope. Just three-on-three today. Let's play."

We played for close to an hour before the clouds starting moving in. Blake and Malik wanted to play another round, but I wanted to return the book to the library before the rain came.

I didn't know when it was due, but I didn't want the book to be late so I'd end up in jail. I said my good-byes and jogged out of the park and up the street to the library. I entered the library doors and almost ran into Caden, who was leaving.

"Baker, watch yourself," he said.

"Sorry," I said.

"What's in your hand?"

"*The Giver.* I'm returning it."

"That's what I need. I'll take that," he said. He swiped the book from my hands.

"I need to return it first."

"It's fine, I'll bring it to school Monday." He smiled. I couldn't tell if he was being honest. I started to focus, but as I concentrated on his mind, he took a step for the doors.

"Where are you going?" I said, losing my focus.

"Thanks, Charlie!" He nodded with a half grin and left the library with my book.

Hot diggity dog! What if he doesn't return the book when he's done? I spun around and exited the library, chasing after him, expecting the siren to go off again. It didn't, but the sky was darker than five minutes before when I'd entered the building. I saw Caden get on his bike and pedal away. I had no shot of catching him.

I guess I will find out what happens if you don't return a book.

I felt a drop of rain on my face. I didn't have much time to make it home before the downpour began, so I started running. The rain started to come down harder when I was about two blocks from home, so I sprinted the last stretch and made it inside my house before I got soaked. I slammed the door shut and collapsed out of breath on the couch.

"Did you get to play today?" my dad asked. He was on his laptop at the table.

"Yes," I said between breaths. "Blake told me I should try out for the basketball team at the school."

"I don't know about that, Charlie. Remember when you got hit with the football at school? You were lucky that no one saw the blue blood dripping from your nose."

"That was Caden's fault. I haven't got hurt once at the park."

"Maybe, but you never know what could happen, especially with the whole school watching."

"The whole school would watch us play?"

"I don't know, maybe? Lots of people go to the high school football games here."

"True."

"You really like basketball?"

"I like playing with the guys at the park."

"When are the tryouts?"

"Blake says they will be at the end of October."

"Good. We have some time to figure it out."

"Thanks, Dad."

"No guarantees."

"I know. And Dad, I might be going to jail soon."

Four

"Did you get the English assignment done?" Maya asked. We were standing at our lockers Monday morning.

"Yep, but I had a run-in with Caden at the library."

"Oh pug," she said.

A big grin spread across my face. "You said 'oh pug'! That was awesome."

"I'm spending too much time with you." She chuckled to herself. "Caden?"

"I went to return *The Giver* and ran into him at the entrance of the library. He took the book before I could return it. He said he'd bring it back today."

"He didn't shove you into a bookshelf or something like that?"

"Nope."

"Did he say anything about Mr. Goshen?"

"Nope. What if he doesn't give back the book? I don't want to go to jail."

Maya burst out laughing. "Jail? If you don't return a book? Where did you get that idea?"

"The siren went off when I tried to leave the library without checking the book out properly, so I thought you went to jail if you don't return books."

She laughed louder.

"Have you heard that siren?"

"No, I don't steal books from the library."

"I don't either! At least not on purpose. That siren was the worst noise ever!"

Maya kept laughing.

"What happens if you don't return a book?"

"No jail. You have to pay for the book if you lose it."

"Hot diggity dog! That's it? Then why the siren?"

"I have no idea."

"I feel better now about Caden taking the book." The first bell rang. "Ready for math?"

"Let's go," she said.

We took our seats in the front of the class. Caden arrived halfway through class with a pass. When class ended, I approached him as we entered the hallways.

"Caden, can I have the book back?"

"What book?" he asked.

"*The Giver*, the one you took from me at the library. Do you have it?"

"Don't worry about it. I'll return it later this week. I won't ruin your perfect library record."

I focused on him quickly and read his thoughts. He was telling the truth. I couldn't believe it.

"Is it true that Goshen sent you to the principal's office last week?" he asked.

"Yes," I replied. Caden smirked and then walked away. I looked behind me. Maya was waiting.

"Did you hear that?" I said. "Caden is going to return the book."

"I doubt it."

"No, he was being honest. Trust me."

"Maybe. But what if he tells Mr. Goshen that you don't have a book to get you in trouble?" she said.

"I doubt it."

Maya looked away, disappointed.

The bell rang.

"I'll see you later," I said. She walked away without a word, but as English class approached, I started to feel anxious about Mr. Goshen, Caden, and even Principal Stevens. I was so nervous that I skipped lunch and hung out at the library, reading over my assignment on *The Giver* and reworking a few answers. When it was time to go to English class, I felt a little better.

"Please hand in your assignments and take out your book." I looked around the room as my classmates pulled out their copies of *The Giver*. I handed my paper up to the front and took a notebook out. I put my arms on my desk to shield it from Mr. Goshen's view. Mr. Goshen began asking the class questions about the book. He called on students at random, so I hoped he wouldn't call on me.

"Charlie, can you read the first paragraph of chapter two? It's on page fourteen."

Lickity split. I turned to Amy, who sat next to me. Her blonde hair and blue eyes were in stark contrast to my dark hair and eyes. I knew she was a friend of Maya, but we hadn't talked much. It was worth a shot.

"Can I borrow your book?" I whispered with a smile. Without hesitation, she handed the book to me. I didn't know if Mr. Goshen saw the exchange, so I waited for him to say something.

"Charlie?" I looked up at the teacher. "Are you going to read?" *Maybe Mr. Goshen didn't see.*

I started reading.

"Okay, stop there. Where is your book?"

"Hot Spaghetti," I mumbled. "I don't have one."

"Did you read the book and complete the assignment?"

"Yes."

"Then where is the book?"

"I let someone borrow it."

"I suggest you get it back for tomorrow's class unless you want to visit Principal Stevens again."

"Okay," I said.

He asked me about the portion we'd just read. Luckily, I knew the answer. He moved on to the next student, so I handed the book back to Amy. When class ended, I turned to Amy.

"Thanks again for letting me borrow your book. It was really nice of you."

"No problem." She smiled. "Did you say 'Hot Spaghetti' earlier?"

"Yes."

"Why did you say that?"

"It's a saying I like."

"I've never heard that before."

"That's because I made it up."

She looked at me with her eyebrows raised. "I need to get to my next class," she said.

"Me too." We turned in opposite directions, and I almost ran into Maya. We walked together for a moment and then stopped at our lockers.

"I almost got sent to the principal's office for not having the book."

"Really?"

"He didn't care that Caden didn't have a book," she said.

"Really? How come I got in trouble then?" I asked.

She looked at me. I wanted to read her mind, but I already knew what she was thinking. Mr. Goshen and Caden were working together against me somehow.

We shut our lockers and went to history class. Caden sneered when I walked past. Maya and I sat in our seats.

"Did you see the look on Caden's face?" I asked.

She nodded. "It was like he knew that you'd get in trouble for not having the book."

"That's not good."

Five

The next morning I arrived at school with a brand-new copy of *The Giver* from the local bookstore. I said hello to Maya and Amy, who were talking at Maya's locker. They smiled back at me. Amy whispered something, and Maya giggled. In that moment, every part of me wanted to read their minds, but I knew I shouldn't. I walked away.

Nothing out of the ordinary happened during my morning classes, but I was worried about gym class. I didn't want to go to the locker room and face Caden. When he teased me at the start of school, he put my clothes in the toilet. I didn't want that to happen again—or something worse.

Before I entered the locker room, I took a deep breath. Caden wasn't at his gym locker, so I went to the last row of lockers to change clothes. I heard him enter the locker room with Jordan. I finished changing and crept closer, but I kept out of sight so I could hear them talking.

"Mr. Goshen is the worst teacher. I'm going to fail his class," Jordan said.

"No, he's not. I don't know what your problem is with him," Caden said.

"We are all going to fail his class." Jordan said. I focused on Caden. For some reason, I could read him easier than most people. One of Caden's memories flashed in my brain. He got an A on the *The Giver* assignment. That didn't seem right. I searched a little deeper, looking for a memory or a thought about Mr. Goshen or me.

"What are you doing, Charlie?" Caden asked, staring at me. I was so focused on mind reading that I didn't realize I had walked around the corner into sight and was staring at them. I probably looked like a zombie to them.

"Going to gym," I said.

"The door is the other way."

"Right," I said. *Oh booger. I look stupid again.* I backtracked and went out the door into the gym.

Maya stood next to Amy with her arms crossed and a frown on her face. She was upset. I didn't know if I should, but I walked up to her.

"What's wrong?" I asked.

"She got sent to the principal's office," Amy said.

"Hot diggity dog!"

"Huh?" Amy said.

"Ignore him," Maya said.

"What happened?" I asked.

"I got a C- on the assignment for English," Maya said. "My parents are going to be so mad," she said.

"It will be okay," Amy said. "It sounds like everybody did bad on the assignment. I'm sure there will be a chance to make up the points."

"Not everybody did bad. Caden got an A," I said.

"Seriously?"

I nodded.

"That can't be fair. There's no way he did better than me. He didn't even buy the book!" Maya said.

"I didn't buy the book either. That doesn't mean he didn't read it," I mumbled.

"Sorry, I didn't mean it like that," she said.

The whistle blew. We followed Mr. Wells's instructions and started learning the rules of volleyball. Then we spent the rest of class "bumping" and "setting" the ball back and forth. Every time I tried to bump it, the ball sailed opposite from the way I intended. When Amy got tired of watching me chase the ball, she showed me how to bump the ball properly. She played on the volleyball team, so I believed her, even if it hurt my arms to hit it this way. I let the ball land on my forearms.

"You must be getting an A on the volleyball team," I said to Amy. She scrunched her face.

"You don't get graded for playing a school sport," Amy said.

Lickity Split. Come up with something. Fast!

"I know, but if you got a grade, it would be an A." I smiled, but she didn't say anything. *Now she definitely thinks I'm weird.*

We returned to bumping the ball back and forth, but it hurt. *Why did all these sports games include a chance of injury or pain?* When gym ended, my forearms were turning blue, but at least I hit the ball back to Amy and Maya successfully four times.

When it was time for English class, I expected the worst from Mr. Goshen. He handed back our assignments first thing. A "D" was scribbled across the top of my paper in red ink. I looked through the assignment, but there were no comments, just a few red x's. At least it wasn't an F.

I glanced over at Amy's paper. She had a C- like Maya. I looked throughout the room and glanced at the papers of my nearby classmates. They had D's and F's too. It looked like Amy's C- was the best grade in our class.

At the end of class, Mr. Goshen announced a test on Thursday.

Is he going to fail everyone while Mrs. Felder was away?

When I saw Maya again in history class, her glum attitude was gone. I turned to face her.

"You're in a better mood," I said.

"I wasn't sure before, but this is it. This is your chance to use your ability to help the school."

"Right now? On who?"

"Charlie, Maya, quiet please," Mrs. Roberts said. I waited until Mrs. Roberts finished her lesson before turning around again.

"So?" I asked.

Maya spoke in a whisper. "We have to get a new sub for Mrs. Felder."

"Why am I getting Mrs. Felder a sandwich?"

Maya cracked up. It took her a few minutes to stop laughing and speak. "Not a sandwich. A new substitute teacher for Mrs. Felder. You can use your special powers to find a way to get Mr. Goshen out of his position."

"A sub. That's right. It's short for substitute teacher."

"What do you think?"

"Why do we need to do that?"

"Mr. Goshen is impossible. Most of the grade is failing, except for Caden. That's not right."

"What is the plan?"

"I don't know yet, but we have to do something." Maya's eyes were wide open, and I could tell she was determined to carry this out somehow. I couldn't let her down.

"Maybe I can help."

"I'll take maybe." She jumped in the air and did a little spin.

"What now?" I asked.

"I have no idea."

"Oh, booger."

"'Oh, booger' again? Let me guess—another one of your new sayings."

I grinned. She shook her head.

"What?" I asked.

"I liked 'oh pug' better."

"That's because you have a pug. But I can't keep saying that because I understand pugs now."

"Understand pugs?"

"Yes. It's what's different about them that makes them cute—the wrinkles and smashed face."

"And curly tails," Maya added.

"Right."

We walked through the hallway and into the gym. The volleyball team was gathering for practice. We circled the edge of the gym to the doors outside. Mr. Goshen entered the gym from the opposite hallway with Caden. They laughed together. I looked at Maya.

She pushed open the doors outside. When the doors slammed shut behind us, she stopped.

"Did you see that?"

"Caden and Mr. Goshen laughing?"

"Yep."

"I have a bad feeling about all of this," she said. "Mr. Goshen, Caden, it doesn't look good for you."

"You have a bad feeling? Can you read minds too?"

"Not yet," she said.

"Wait, is there something you aren't telling me?" I asked.

She cracked up.

"Lickity split. You were joking."

We walked through the field. The leaves had started to turn an array of red, orange, and yellow. A few drifted through the air as we walked on the trail through the woods.

"Do you really think Caden and Mr. Goshen are working together against me?"

"Maybe. We need to keep our eyes on them … and maybe your mind."

"Eyes on them? That means pay attention to them, right?"

"Yep."

"Hey, I finally got a saying right!" I grinned, but inside I worried that Maya was right about Caden and Mr. Goshen.

Six

Maya and I didn't have a chance to come up with a plan for the rest of the week. We were sidetracked by Thursday's English test, so we spent most of Wednesday evening studying *The Giver*. Maya reread the entire book, but we didn't study enough. When we took the test on Thursday, each of us turned in our tests knowing we hadn't done well.

Friday morning, Maya and I barely spoke. She was nervous about getting her test back, and since she had English during second period, she would know first. When I saw her at the beginning of gym class, I knew it wasn't good.

"What did you get on your test?" I asked as Mr. Wells broke us into teams for volleyball.

Amy, Maya, and I were placed on the same team.

"I got another C on my English test. I studied for that test. I knew everything, but he took points off on all my short answer questions."

"I'm sorry."

"Everybody did bad again. Well, mostly everybody," Amy said. "I can't believe Caden got an A."

"He did?" I asked.

"Yes, he was bragging about it in the hallway," Maya said.

"I don't believe him," Amy said.

"Charlie, you should double-check that he's telling the truth, by, you know ..." Maya said.

"By what?" Amy asked.

"Mind reading," I said without thinking.

Amy started laughing. "No, really, how?"

"I'll see if I can find his test in the locker room."

"Oh," Amy said. "Have you done something like that before?" she asked with a smile.

"Not exactly," I said. The truth was I didn't want to read his mind because I was trying to stay away from him.

"First six on the court. The rest can line up on the sideline," Mr. Wells shouted. Amy, Maya, and I stepped on to the court. The ball sailed over the net. Without thinking I caught it. *Lickity split.*

"You're not supposed to catch it," Maya said.

"I know. I didn't mean to."

The next ball sailed over the net right to me. This time the ball hit my clenched hands and went sailing to the right.

"Out of bounds," Mr. Wells called.

"Caden is aiming for you," Maya said. I looked up to see Caden serve the ball again. This time I successfully bumped the ball back over the net. A girl on the other team missed the hit, so we got the ball back. I moved into the serving position. We hadn't practiced serving.

"Do you know how to serve the ball?" Amy asked.

"No," I said. A teammate passed me the ball. Amy showed me the underhand motion to serve.

I put the ball in my left hand, swung my right arm backward, and then forward as fast as I could. The ball sailed high into the air and dropped on our side of the net.

"Charlie, you can try one more time," Mr. Wells said.

This time the ball sailed over the net. I breathed a sigh of relief. For the remainder of the game, I didn't have any more goofs.

Back in the locker room, I changed quickly and then went to the front where Caden and Jordan were talking. I pretended like I was washing my hands, and I listened to their conversation. It had nothing to do with English. I had to do this the hard way. I circled back to my backpack in my locker bay and grabbed it.

When I returned to the front of the locker room, Caden and Jordan were at the mirrors; their folders were on the bench. I inched closer and saw a paper sticking out of Caden's folder. I hurried, opened it, and saw that it was an A on the English test. I closed the folder and stood as they turned around to face me. I walked past them with a smile and went to class. Mission successful.

My test grade was worse than I expected. I thought I had studied enough to earn a C, but I was a wrong. "D" was inked in red pen at the top of my test, and after looking through the test, I didn't understand why I got answers wrong. But then again, I didn't really understand the English language. I told Maya about my test and Caden's test score at the end of the school day.

"Are you thinking what I'm thinking?" I said.

"You're the one who can read minds!"

"Right." I focused on her and an image of Caden and Mr. Goshen came into focus. "You think ..."

"Hey! I didn't tell you to read my mind!" she said, interrupting me.

"Hot Spaghetti, I'm sorry! I didn't realize—"

"That I was joking," Maya said, finishing my thought. "Caden is the only student that I know got an A. I don't know of anyone else who has received a grade above a C. Even Erin hasn't gotten an A or a B on any assignment or test in his class. She is the smartest kid in our grade."

"What do we do?"

"We need to tell the principal. Will you come with me Monday morning before school?"

"Is that a good idea? The principal doesn't like me."

"I need you there to read his mind so we know what to do."

"I don't know ..."

"Please, Charlie." She stared at me, and I knew I couldn't say no.

"I'll be there," I mumbled. We stood in awkward silence, trying to figure out what to say, when Amy walked up to us.

"Do you want to come with us to a corn maze tomorrow? My mom can fit one more in her minivan."

"Are you talking to me?" I asked.

"You should come, Charlie," Amy said. "My brother is coming with one of his friends. You won't be the only boy."

"Okay," I said. The real problem was I didn't know what she meant by corn maze.

"Cool. Can you come to my house at one tomorrow afternoon?"

"Sure."

She gave me the address to her house and told me to bring ten dollars. Her house was far from mine.

"Can you pick me up?" I asked Maya. "It's a long walk, and I think my Dad has a meeting tomorrow. We only have one car."

"My mom is already mad at me for English. If I ask for anything else, she might not let me go," Maya said.

"Ride your bike, it won't take that long. I've ridden to Maya's before, and you two live close to each other," Amy said.

"Bike?" I mumbled.

"See you tomorrow! I need to catch my bus." Amy waved and left down the hallway.

"Bike?" I asked Maya again.

"Bike—you know, two wheels, you pedal."

"Hot Spaghetti! Oh right, I knew that. I'll ask my dad for one. Are they easy to learn how to operate?"

"Riding a bike is simple. You'll be fine."

"Great!" Then I remembered Maya said checking out a book was simple, and that turned out to be wrong.

Seven

On my way home, my mind was racing with everything that happened during the week. I didn't know what to do about Caden, Mr. Goshen, the principal, or even this corn maze. I didn't want to meet with the principal, let alone read his mind. He clearly didn't like me. *What if I mess up while I'm in his head?*

When I entered my house, I felt my parents' presence in my head, and in a matter of seconds, they knew everything. My mom and dad met me in the living room.

"I don't know what to do," I told my dad.

"If you think Mr. Goshen is being unfair, talking with the principal is a great idea. He might be able to help you or give you some advice," my mother said.

"But you shouldn't use mind reading while talking with someone," my father said. "It's easy to respond to a thought by accident, and you don't know how someone will react if you respond to them in their head or answer a question they didn't ask. It could cause trouble. We don't want that right now."

"I won't get myself into hot mud again."

"What?"

"Hot mud—doesn't that mean getting into trouble?"

"I think the saying is hot water, not hot mud."

"Oh, booger."

"I thought you were going to study the English language more," my mother said.

"I haven't had the chance. I've been busy."

"Yes, busy getting stuck in hot mud," my dad replied, laughing at his own joke. "But, you know the rules. You are to avoid mind reading on humans, especially when in conversation with them."

I knew they were right, so that meant I needed to lie to Maya or not help her with Mr. Goshen. Neither was a good option.

"What's this about a bike and a corn maze?" my mom asked.

"Can I go to a corn maze with friends tomorrow? Maya and Amy asked me to go with them."

"What's a corn maze?" my mom asked.

"I don't know."

"It's a popular fall activity," my dad said. "He will be fine."

"But what is it?" I asked.

"You'll find out." My dad grinned. *Oh pug.* My dad and mom were staring at each other, grinning, so apparently my mom knew about a corn maze now. I could look it up later. I had another plan for tonight.

"Can I have a bike?"

"Is that the thing with two wheels?" my mom asked.

"Yes, you pedal it to go forward."

"Interesting," my mom said.

"Yes, I've seen kids riding bikes," my dad added.

"Maya says to get one."

"Any risks?" my mom asked.

"Not that I know of," I said. My dad agreed.

"Can we go get one at the store?"

"I don't see why not," my dad said. He grabbed his keys. "Let's go now, before dinner."

We arrived at the sports store and found the bikes in the back. I picked out a bike that looked like Blake's. A teenage boy with shaggy brown hair came over to us.

"You can test ride it through the aisles," he said.

I pulled it out in the aisle and sat on the seat with my feet touching the ground.

"All I do is pedal?" I asked my dad.

"I think so," my dad said. The sales guy gave us a weird look. I put my feet on the pedals, but before I could start to pedal, the bike and I started to lean to one side. I was falling.

"Lickity split!" I said as I put my feet down to brace myself before I fell.

"Have you ridden a bike before?" the shaggy hair guy asked me.

"Yes," I said. I have no idea why I lied. My dad glared at me. I ignored him. *Maybe if I pedal faster.*

I took a deep breath, put my feet on the pedals, and started pedaling.

I am doing it! I am moving! I am riding a bike!

I looked up and saw my aisle was ending. I needed to turn or stop. I had no idea how to stop, but maybe I could turn. I kept pedaling, afraid to stop. As the bike went faster, I started to turn the handlebars, but it was too late. The bike didn't turn as fast I thought it would. I slammed into an aisle of shoes and fell to the left, with the bike and boxes of shoes landing on me.

"Oh booger," I whimpered.

"Charlie, are you okay?" my dad said, jogging over to me. Then he entered my head. *Did you break any skin?*

I don't know.

I started to move, pushing the boxes off of me as my dad lifted the bike. I glanced over my body. I felt a tingling on my leg where the pedal had fallen on me.

I think my leg, I told my dad through my head.

Go to the car. I'll take care of the bike, my dad told me in my head. He handed me the keys when I stood. I sprinted out of the store and into the car.

"I'm so sorry," I heard my dad say as I started to run. I got in the car and sat in the front. I rolled my pant leg up. A stream of blue ran down my leg. I found a bottle of water in the cup holder and a few napkins in the glove box. I poured some water on my leg until the blue stopped seeping and the scrape healed. I wiped the blue off my leg and rolled my pant leg down. Then I waited.

Ten minutes later, my dad walked out, rolling the bicycle. He put it in the in back of our car.

"I'm sorry," I said.

"It's okay. How's your leg?"

"Fine."

"Good."

"I didn't realize you could hurt yourself."

"Me either."

"You need to make sure you can do this if I let you keep the bike."

"I'll practice at home."

"You have to be an expert before you take this bike out. What if that worker at the store saw your leg?"

"He didn't, Dad."

"This time, Charlie. I don't know. You are worrying me—basketball, bike riding, and using your ability on humans."

"I'm sorry. I'm trying. It's hard," I said.

I felt my dad in my head. He gave me a sense of peace and forgiveness. *It's okay. We all mess up. Our family will figure out this Earth thing together.*

Eight

After spending an hour researching corn mazes on the internet Saturday morning, I had a better idea of what to expect, but I didn't quite get the concept. *Why did I want to get lost?* I asked my mom, but she couldn't give me any more answers. My dad had left for his yoga class, so he couldn't help either. I couldn't believe he was still taking yoga, but he said it was relaxing, and he learned a lot about Silver Lake from the people in the class.

I decided to walk to Amy's house instead of risking a bike catastrophe. I started the half-hour walk, leaving with way more time than I needed. After taking one wrong turn, I needed the extra time to make it to Amy's house. Maya arrived a few minutes later.

"Ready for this? A day with the girls?" Maya asked with a smile.

"I thought I wasn't the only boy."

"Amy's brother is eight. I don't think you will be running through the corn maze with him."

"You run through the corn maze?"

"No, my stupid brother probably will," Amy said, exiting her front door. Her mother followed, along with the two young boys. The blond-haired, blue-eyed boy had to be Amy's sister.

"Hi, I'm Charlie." I greeted James, Amy's brother, and Brandon, his friend, before I introduced myself to her mom, Mrs. Kleft. We loaded up the minivan, and within minutes I fell asleep. I didn't mean to, but the van was warm, and the motion soothed me. When I closed my eyes, I imagined myself on Europa, flying around in a pod with my family. I woke up to the slight jerk of the van stopping. We were in a gravel parking lot next to a large, red barn.

"Tired?" Maya asked. I nodded.

We walked in and paid five dollars to a man seated behind a table. We each received a red wristband and a map. I inspected the wristband, wondering if there was a tracking device in case we got lost in the maze. I couldn't tell.

"I'm going to stay with the boys. Amy, call if you need to," her mom said.

We walked through the barn and out the other side. Corn stalks were everywhere, but I saw a small clearing with a path leading into the corn. A man stood next to it. Maya and Amy flashed their wristbands at him, so I did likewise. Then we walked on the path into the corn maze. Amy and Maya talked nonstop while I stared at the corn surrounding us. All I could see was corn. It was a little creepy, and I had a million questions for Amy and Maya about the maze. But I didn't what to sound stupid, so I kept my questions to myself. I knew that trails were cut into the corn stalks, and we had to find our way through it. That was enough.

When we hit a section where the path diverged in two, Maya took out her map. "I think we go this way," she said, pointing to the right.

"What if you're wrong?" I asked, looking at the map. I didn't quite understand where we were on the map.

"Then we spend more time walking in the maze," she said.

"Don't we want to spend more time in the maze? Isn't that why we are here?" I said.

Amy laughed.

"You're funny," she said. I didn't know how to respond, so I grinned. We started walking and talking again. Soon Mr. Goshen came up in our conversation.

"He's the worst teacher," Maya said.

"Everybody is going to fail his class," Amy added. We came to another crossroads.

"We are going to talk to the principal Monday about him so the principal will do something about Mr. Goshen."

"Do what?" Amy asked.

"I don't know. Maybe talk to Mr. Goshen, or get a new teacher for Mrs. Felder."

"Do you think that will work?"

"Maybe. It's worth a try."

"Charlie, you are going, too?" Amy asked.

I nodded. We paused at the next intersection.

"Which way, Charlie?" Amy asked.

"Oh, booger," I said. "Right?"

Maya had her map out again. "No, I think it's to the left."

"Let's go left. Charlie, you go right. Let's see who makes it out first," Amy said.

"I don't know," I said, looking at Maya, pleading with her. She knew I had a bad sense of direction.

"Maybe we should stick together. That's what your mom said," Maya said.

"That's no fun. Come on!" Amy pulled Maya left and started jogging down the trail. "See you later, Charlie!"

"Lickity split." I pulled out my map, but I had no idea where we were. I crumpled it up and put it in my pocket. I tried to focus on Maya, but I couldn't locate her. I sensed a few other people, but again, not enough to help. I began to walk down the path, trying to get my bearings. I didn't like being alone in the corn, and Amy said we were racing. *I better hurry up.* I began to jog. At the next intersection, I went right. *If I go right every time, I have to make it out eventually.*

After the fourth right turn, I stopped. I was lost. I needed to use my ability. I listened and heard some people in the distance. I couldn't see them anywhere. I concentrated all my energy on one voice, and I did it!

I was in someone's head, even though I couldn't see him. He was through the corn on the right. *We are almost out. I think it's just a few minutes down the path*, said the voice in my head. I looked at the corn, took a deep breath, and started through it.

I ducked and pushed my way through the tall corn stalks, staying focused on whoever I could sense. Ahead, something small scurried in front of me.

"Hot Spaghetti!" I yelled. Then I saw some light through the corn. *A clearing!* I pushed through the last corn stalks and stumbled on to the path in front of Caden and Jordan. *Caden! I was in Caden's head again?*

"Baker, what are you doing?"

"Corn maze," I said.

"Are you lost, loser?" Caden asked.

"Everybody is lost. Isn't that the point of the maze?" I asked.

"Real funny," Caden said.

"Let's go," Jordan said.

I saw it coming, but I couldn't stop it in time. Caden shoved me, and I stumbled and fell on my butt to the dirt ground. Caden and Jordan walked away.

"Charlie?" Amy's mom approached me from a few feet away. My clothes were covered in dirt.

"Hi," I said with a half smile. She lent me a hand.

"Are you okay?" she asked.

"Yes." I brushed off some of the dirt.

"What happened?"

"I stumbled and fell."

"Where are Amy and Maya?"

"I don't know. They told me to go another way. I got lost."

"Oh dear."

"I bet they finished," I said.

"Come on, let's keep going. I think this is the last stretch." As we walked, the boys whipped each other with leaves from the corn stalks. A few minutes later, I saw an open field and the red barn behind it.

"Hot diggity dog," I said.

"What did you say?" asked Amy's mom.

"Nothing."

"Don't worry, I won't tell them you got lost," Amy's mom said.

"Thanks." We entered the red barn. I expected to see Amy and Maya, but they weren't there yet. The delicious smell of popcorn entered my Earthly senses.

"Is there popcorn here?"

"I think they have snacks over there." She pointed to a table across the barn.

"I'll be right back," I said. I ran over to the snack bar and spent my remaining five dollars on the five boxes of popcorn. I opened one box and held it in the air in front of my mouth, pouring the popcorn in it. When I finished, the woman working the snack bar was staring at me. I hurried away with my remaining four boxes. I probably shouldn't have eaten the popcorn so fast.

Maya and Amy were standing with Amy's mom. I waved and joined them.

"You beat us!" Maya said. "I can't believe it. You are terrible with directions."

"I got lucky."

"Is that popcorn for us?" Amy asked.

"Yes," I said, knowing that wasn't the original plan, but Amy smiled at me as I handed her a box.

"I'll split it with Maya," she said, and then she looked at her brother and his friend. *Does she want me to give up the other box too?* I knew I shouldn't, but I jumped inside Amy's head. *Yes, she wants me to give the popcorn to her brother. Then she* was *thinking about me. What?* I jumped out of her head. I shouldn't be in there.

"Here's one for you two," I said, handing the box to James and Brandon.

We loaded into the car. I ate my two boxes, wishing there were four like I had planned.

When we got back to Amy's house, I sat with them out on Amy's porch waiting for Maya to get picked up.

"Why does everyone like corn mazes here?" I asked.

"It's fun getting lost and trying to find your way out," Maya said.

"I don't think so."

"What is fun for you?" Amy asked.

"I don't know what's fun for me on Earth." Maya's eyes widened. *Lickity Split.* "I like playing basketball with the guys at the park," I said, trying to recover past my goof.

"You play basketball?" Amy asked.

I hope she missed my Earth comment. "Yes. Why is everyone surprised that I play?"

Amy giggled. "Nothing." I looked to Maya.

"We've seen you play football and kickball in gym class," Maya said.

"Not the kickball thing again. I'm going to hear about that until the end of the clock!"

"I think you mean time," Maya said.

"Did you two see Caden and Jordan in the maze?" I asked.

They shook their heads. "Did you?" Maya asked.

"We ran into each other," I said.

"And, did you ...?"

"Nope. Nothing happened," I said.

"You didn't try to—"

A black SUV pulled into the driveway before Maya could finish her question.

"See you Monday," Maya said. "You can fill me in then, Charlie." I nodded. She got into the car with her mom. Her mom smiled at us, and then they left.

"I'm glad you came today," Amy said. "I had fun with you, even if you say weird things."

"I do?"

"Yes."

"I better go now." I stood and waved good-bye to Amy as I walked home. She smiled and waved. I felt my cheeks warm, so I turned around before my face was completely blue. *Why is that happening?* I walked home confused, thinking about Amy and Maya.

Nine

I parked my bike at the rack outside the front doors of the school. Even though I'd practiced riding my bike the whole day before, I was relieved to make it to the school without falling.

I hurried into the empty school and met Maya at our lockers.

"I'll do the talking," she said. "You do your thing."

We walked to the office, and the secretary had us sit down and wait. The principal brought us into his office a few minutes later.

"What can I do for you two?" he asked.

"We want to talk to you about Mr. Goshen. He's not fair. Everybody is getting bad grades except for Caden Garfield."

"And?"

"It's not right. He can't do that. We are working hard, and Caden isn't."

"Do you have any proof that anything Mr. Goshen is doing is unfair?"

Maya bit her lip. I stared at the ceiling.

"Sometimes you have to earn a good grade. You can't walk into class and expect to get an A," he said. His facial expression did not change.

"I don't!" she said. "It's not just me. Charlie is failing. Even Erin Donofrio is getting C's! She's the smartest girl in our grade. You have to get a new sub for Mrs. Felder."

"A C is not failing," he said.

"Mr. Stevens, can you at least talk to Mr. Goshen and ask him how we can do better?" I asked.

"As a student, you need to ask your teacher these questions, not me. You may go now," he said.

Lickity split. We have nothing. Should I try? My parents probably won't approve. I looked at Maya and then back to Principal Stevens. *I have to try for her.*

Suddenly I was in his head. *I'm not bringing in a new teacher because two students think Mr. Goshen is hard*, he was thinking.

Hot Spaghetti, how did I get in the Principal Steven's head so quickly? I barely tried.

Maya stood to leave. I stood with her.

Get out of my head, Mr. Stevens thought.

I shuddered and looked at Mr. Stevens. He was staring at me. I stood from the chair and left the room as quickly as I could. Maya followed me into the hallway. I walked halfway across the school before I stopped and leaned against the lockers.

"Are you okay?"

"Yes," I said. *What just happened? I need to go home and tell my parents right away.*

"Charlie ... Charlie ..."

"What?"

"What was the principal thinking?"

"He's not going to do anything because Mrs. Felder will be back in two months."

"I guess we have to come up with another plan then," she said.

"A plan?"

"To get Mr. Goshen to quit."

"Yeah," I said, but my mind was elsewhere. My head was pounding. *I need to get out of here. I need to go home.*

"Charlie, Charlie ... are you okay?" I opened my eyes and looked at Maya.

"I need to go home," I said. I slammed my locker and dashed out the front doors of the school. I pedaled home as fast as I could, nearly wiping out on the turn to my street. The car wasn't in the driveway. I burst through the front door to an empty house.

I paced throughout the house, replaying all my conversations with Principal Stevens. When I was sent to the office the first time at the beginning of the year, I had tried to read his mind. His mind was completely blank. I had thought that was weird, but today he knew I was in his head. And he responded to me in my head! *Is he a special human with powers, or is he an alien like me? Is he from Europa?* Nothing made sense, and my parents weren't home.

I picked up the phone to call my dad when I heard the garage door open. Immediately, our minds connected, and he knew everything from the conversation with the principal before he got out of the car. I felt his concern about Principal Stevens. That made me more anxious. He entered the house and sat with me in the living room.

"We know there are other aliens on Earth," he said.

"I know that some other Europan families escaped here. Principal Stevens isn't part of one of those families, right?"

"Correct."

"Who is he? Is he Europan?"

"I don't know, son. I'll connect with the other Europan families we know on Earth to see if they know him."

"What do we do?"

"You do nothing. Charlie, stay away from your principal for now."

"I don't know if I can do that."

"Why?"

"Mr. Goshen might be plotting against me."

"Really?"

"I don't know. Maya thinks that might be true, and she wants to find a way to get a better teacher to replace Mrs. Felder while she's away."

"Charlie, this sounds like a bad idea."

"What is a bad idea?"

"All of it. Do you understand what you are doing?"

"Helping a friend?" I said with a smile.

My dad sighed. "I know you are trying to help Maya, but trying to get a teacher removed isn't the best idea."

"But what do I do then? I want to help Maya."

"I don't know, son, but I trust that you will make the right decision. And Charlie, for now, no mind reading during school."

"At all? What if—"

"Try to avoid it until we figure out Principal Stevens."

"Okay. Should I go back to school?"

"Yes, I'll drive you so you don't get in trouble."

We loaded into the car, and a few minutes later I was back at school. Before I got out of the car, my dad stopped me.

"Charlie, let's not tell Maya about Principal Stevens. We don't know what we are dealing with, and I don't want to take unnecessary risks."

"I thought you said the only other aliens on Earth were Europans."

"I did."

"But?"

"Charlie, let me take care of this," he said, cutting me off.

"Okay, Dad." I opened the door and waved good-bye.

When I entered the school, I hurried to the office with my note, hoping not to run into

Principal Stevens again. I handed my note to the secretary. She wrote a pink slip, and I was out the door before Principal Stevens knew I was there. Maybe he didn't know, I couldn't be sure.

"You're back," Maya said when I entered math class. She was working on today's lesson. I had made it back for the last ten minutes of class. "Is everything okay?"

"Yes, sorry, I wasn't feeling well, but I'm better now."

"Are you sure?"

"Yes. It's an alien virus thing. I'm fine," I said. I smiled to reassure her, but I felt bad about not telling her about the principal. I didn't like keeping the truth from her, even for a good reason.

"I have the perfect plan," she said.

"Let's hear it," I said.

"We have to get more kids and their parents involved," she said. "As many as possible."

"Why?"

"Because the principal will have to listen if it's most of the kids and their parents. If parents call him and tell him that Mr. Goshen is a horrible teacher, he has to listen."

"Okay, that makes sense, but how do we get parents and kids to do that?"

"We tell our friends to tell their parents what's happening in Mr. Goshen's class."

"I hate to break it to you, but you're the only friend I have. This is all on you."

"You can help. Watch and learn."

We wandered through the halls until we found two girls chatting at their locker. I stayed back a bit while Maya entered their conversation.

"Did you hear that Erin got a C on the English test?"

"No way!"

"Yes. Me, too."

"I got a D."

"Mr. Goshen is so hard."

"We are all going to flunk his class."

"He can't do that to everyone. Tell your parents to complain to the principal. Maybe if enough parents complain, he will have to change how he grades, or maybe Mrs. Felder will come back earlier."

"Yeah! Thanks for the idea, Maya." Maya walked back to me with a grin on her face.

"Did you hear that?"

"Yes."

"See if you can do that."

"I'll try."

I bumbled my way through my morning classes, but I didn't have anyone to talk to about Mr. Goshen. When I met up with Maya at the end of the day, she had talked with almost every girl in the sixth grade. I had told no one. She was confident that her friends would help with her plan, but I didn't think Principal Stevens would change his mind. I began brainstorming other ideas, especially ones that didn't involve the principal. I didn't want to fail English class, but really, I didn't want to let Maya down. I knew that her English grade was really upsetting her. She tried to hide it, but even without reading her mind, she couldn't hide anything from me. I had to help her. I just hoped it didn't involve Principal Stevens.

Ten

The next morning, I sat down in front of Maya in math class. The morning announcements came on over the loud speaker.

"Boys' basketball tryouts will be held in the gym on November 3 and 4 from 3:00 p.m. to 4:30 p.m. Girls' basketball tryouts will be held in the gym on November 3 and 4 from 4:30 p.m. to 6:00 p.m. Please sign up outside of the gym by this Friday if you plan on trying out. Today's lunch is ..." I tuned out and turned around in my chair to face Maya.

"Hot diggity dog! I almost forgot about basketball with the Mr. Goshen and Principal Stevens thing."

"Forgot what exactly?"

"I'm going to try out for the basketball team."

"Really?"

"Yep!"

"Oh," Maya said and looked away.

"What's wrong?" I asked.

"I don't want you to get your hopes up."

"What do you mean?"

"Do you think you can make the team?" she asked.

"Blake says I have a good shot."

"Are you sure he isn't messing with you?"

"What? We don't make a mess together."

"No, messing with you, like playing a joke on you."

"No, we don't joke much. We play basketball together."

"You think Blake is being honest?"

"Yes. We are friends." She looked to the floor. "You don't think I have friends or can play basketball!" I said.

"You aren't supposed to read my mind," she said.

Some students turned our direction. "Watch what you say," I whispered.

"Charlie, I told you not to read my mind."

"I swear I didn't. I could tell from what you said."

"Fine," she said. She didn't believe me and ignored me for the rest of the class. When the bell rang, I spun around, but she rose from her chair and left for the hallway. I followed her, finally catching her when she got stuck in a group of slow-moving sixth graders.

"Maya, what's wrong?"

"Nothing," she said. "I need to go to English. I probably failed another assignment. Later, Charlie."

I could hear the resignation in her voice. *English. Mr. Goshen. Of course.* I watched her walk away from me. I was thinking about a way that I could cheer her up when the bell started to ring.

"Lickity split! I'm late," I said. I dashed across the hallway to science and entered the classroom a few seconds after the bell finished ringing. My science teacher had his back to the class, writing on the board, so I crept to my desk trying not to make a sound. When I sat down, I focused on him. The thoughts of my classmates swirled around, but I concentrated. He was thinking about the lesson on cells. Nothing about me being late. He finished writing on the board and faced the class.

"Charlie Baker, you're late."

"Oh booger," I said. The room started giggling. *I didn't mean to say that out loud.* "I'm sorry." He walked over to his grade book and made a note or mark.

"One more time and you will have detention." He put his pen down on his desk. "Let's get started on the lesson."

A detention for being late? Yikes!

After science class, I stopped at the bulletin board outside the boys' locker room. The sign-up sheet for basketball tryouts was posted on it. I hadn't cleared it with my parents yet, but I wanted to be part of something here on Earth, something that was completely an Earthly thing. Maybe this was how. Mom and Dad would say yes. They'd have to.

I took a pencil from my backpack and put my name on the list. I was the seventh person to sign up.

"Jordan, I'm not sure if you will make the team. Charlie is going to take your spot," Caden said. Jordan and Caden started laughing.

"I beat you at the park that one time," I said.

"No, Blake and Malik beat us."

"They think I will make it," I said, trying to defend myself. They laughed again. "I guess we will see."

"I bet he doesn't even try out," Jordan said as I walked past them to the locker room.

Now I really needed to try out. I couldn't look like I turkeyed out. Or was it chickened?

After I changed into my gym clothes, I saw Maya in the gym talking with Amy. I joined the girls.

"What's wrong?" I asked.

"Nothing," Maya said.

"That's not true."

"Charlie, I don't want to talk right now," Maya said. I looked at Amy, trying to figure out what to do.

"You heard her," Amy said. I looked again at Maya, but she looked down, avoiding my gaze. I could tell she was sad or angry about something. I wanted to know more, so I started to concentrate. *No. I can't.* I walked away.

We played another game of volleyball during gym class. I hit the ball over the net correctly about three out of ten times. I didn't think that was a good percentage.

"See, you can't even play volleyball. You can't hang with us on the basketball court," Caden said as I entered the locker room at the end of class. I ignored him, thinking about Maya. Something was wrong. I didn't know what. Worse, I could find out, but that might hurt her even more.

Maya and I didn't talk much the rest of the day. I got another bad grade in English. When we were at our lockers at the end of the day, Maya told me she was getting picked up from school today, and she left. I wandered in the hallways and found Amy.

"Can you tell me why Maya is upset?"

"No. I don't really know actually. I think it's just Mr. Goshen."

"Did she get a bad grade?"

"I think another C+."

"Did you get a bad grade?"

"I got a C+ too."

"A C isn't that bad, right? Maybe it's not the grades?"

"I don't know, Charlie. She didn't say anything else to me."

"Okay, thanks Amy."

I needed to talk to Maya.

"What is on your mind?" my dad asked when I walked into his office. "Basketball, I see."

"Yes. I'd like to try out."

"I know you've been playing at the park. I've watched some basketball on TV. It seems to be a safe game. Would you agree?"

"Yes."

"But there is running and jumping," he said. I nodded in agreement. "Do you hit each other?" my dad asked.

"Not exactly. If you do, it's a foul, like a penalty."

"So, there is some physical contact."

"Mostly on your arms when you shoot the ball."

"I don't know, son. Bare arms are tricky. What if you get scratched?"

"I've been playing at the playground since the beginning of school, and nothing has happened."

"But this is in front of your school. If something happens, you can't hide it. We can't hide it."

"Nothing will happen, I promise."

"You know you can't promise me that. Life on Earth is random sometimes. Why do you want to play?"

I shrugged, embarrassed by my reasoning. My father entered my head and saw my need for friendship and to fit in at Silver Lake. He saw my interaction with Caden today. He took a deep breath.

"Let me check with your mother. Maybe you can wear long sleeves when you play."

Excitement filled my head. My dad felt it and smiled.

When my mother came home later, they were in deep conversation about me. When they finally called me to their room, they caught me off guard with their question.

"Have you had any more interactions with the principal?"

"No."

"Then join the basketball team."

"Hot diggity dog!" Both of my parents shook their heads. "Wait for it ... you are going to say be careful! I didn't even have to read your mind to know that."

"Yes, Charlie, be careful. This is real important. You can't let anyone see you bleed."

"I know. Thanks!" I ran out of the room and down the stairs.

Where are you going? asked my mom telepathically.

Maya's house. I need to help her with something

Okay. Be home by dinner.

I set my bike in the driveway and looked at Maya's house. It was a single story white house. I walked up to the front door and knocked. A tall, skinny teenage boy answered the door. He towered over me. I heard a low-pitched bark in the background.

"Is Maya home?" I asked. He nodded.

"Maya, some short dude is at the door for you," he shouted.

Maya came into view with a small, light-brown pug at her feet. Her brother stepped away, and the dog ran to me, barking.

"Charlie, what's going on?"

"This is your pug! Can I touch her?"

Maya scooped up her dog, and the barking ceased.

"You can try to pet her, but she doesn't like it."

"You're petting her," I said.

"She only likes me."

"What a funny creature." I touched her fur on her head and neck. The pug sneezed, and the snot hit my face. Maya laughed.

"Charlie, why are you here?"

"I heard you got another C in English."

"Who told you that?"

"Amy."

"What did you get?"

"A C."

"Are your parents mad?" she asked.

"No. They know I'm trying."

"Ugh. Even alien parents understand."

"Understand what?"

"That nobody can get an A in English right now. My parents are on my back. If I don't get an A for this quarter, my parents aren't going to let me play basketball."

"I forgot you play basketball," I said. "Why don't you play with me at the park?"

"I don't know. Maybe because you've never asked me to play."

"Oh," I said, confused and disappointed. "What about your plan?"

"It's been almost a week, and nothing has happened. None of my friends will tell their parents. They are all worried about getting in trouble for their bad grades. They say it will get better."

"We need another plan," I said.

"Like what? We are running out of time."

"I might have an idea."

The pug barked, and Maya looked at me. I told her my plan. She thought it might work, but we needed to start right away. Basketball season was approaching quickly.

Eleven

When the school day ended Friday, I ventured over to Mr. Goshen's classroom. The door was open, so I glanced into the room. He was seated at his desk in the back corner.

The school day was over, so technically I wouldn't be mind reading during school. I took a few steps behind me to be out of his view and concentrated on his location in the room. After a minute or two, I realized it wasn't working. I couldn't get far enough into his head. I only caught glimpses of what he was thinking. I needed to get closer. The only option was to talk to him, but I had to be careful.

"Hi, Mr. Goshen," I said, walking into the room and to his desk.

"Look what the cat dragged in," he said. I scanned the room, but I didn't see any cats.

"Where is the cat?" I asked.

"There is no cat, Charlie. It's a saying."

"I've never heard that one before. What does it mean?"

"What do you think it means?"

"I have no idea. I don't have a cat." He shook his head. I sensed aggravation from him.

"Charlie, why are you here?"

"I want to get better grades. How can I do that?"

"Study."

"I'm doing that."

"Then study more."

"That's it? Can't you give me some pointers or extra help?"

"Normally, yes, but unfortunately, I can't today. I need to leave. Ask your parents or a friend for help, or we can talk Monday before school." He motioned for me to leave the room, but I stood motionless as he gathered a few items from his desk and placed them in his bag.

I am running out of time. I focused on his head. His thoughts were directed at a gym or maybe it was a fitness center. He needed to be ready for the wrestling match this weekend. He stood, grabbed his bag, and left the room. I followed him out of the classroom.

Maya was waiting outside the classroom.

"Did you get anything?"

"Maybe the start of something. He was thinking about working out and getting ready for a wrestling match."

"I don't know how the wrestling thing helps us, and I'm running out of time," Maya said.

"I'll keep trying. I'll go back Monday morning, but I need your help with the English homework. Do you want to come over?"

"Now?"

"Yes."

"All right."

"Great. Then I'll understand a little better when I try to talk to him Monday morning."

We left the school and walked to my house. When we stepped into the driveway, I felt my mother in my head. She asked about Maya through telepathy, and I told her we had homework to do together. I figured she was working in her office, but when I opened the front door, she was waiting for us on the couch in the living room.

"Hi, Maya," she said. "Nice to see you again." She walked over to Maya and gave her a high five. I smacked my face with my palm.

"What?" my mom asked, reading my reaction.

"A high five is a weird greeting," I said.

"I don't think so," Maya said. "I like it."

My mom grinned.

"Nice to see you again." My mom smiled at Maya.

I took Maya to the table, and we sat next to each other. We took out our homework. Maya walked me through the grammar for the assignment, and with her help I had a better understanding of punctuation.

"We still won't get an A. He always finds a reason to dock points," Maya said.

"What did you say, Maya?" my mom asked.

"She was talking about Mr. Goshen. He finds reasons to mark our answers wrong. It's impossible to get a good grade in his class," I said.

"I doubt that," my mom said.

"He's really hard," Maya said.

"This is the worst she's done in a class before," I said. Maya glared at me. "We are trying to get Mrs. Felder to come back." I felt my mom enter my thoughts and see how I used my ability with Mr. Goshen.

"You shouldn't be using your ability in school. Your dad talked to you about this," she said aloud.

"Wait, you aren't allowed to use your ability?" Maya asked.

"My parents don't want me using it in school. You know, cheating and such," I said, leaving out the part about Mr. Stevens.

"That makes sense," she said. "I'm sorry, Mrs. Baker, I didn't know Charlie shouldn't be doing that."

"Thanks, Maya, but what is the big deal about Mr. Goshen? It's been on your mind quite a bit," she said.

"Everyone is failing his class," I said.

"Everyone?" asked my mom.

"It's true, Mrs. Baker. Mr. Goshen gives everyone bad grades and sends students to the principal's office a lot." The mention of Principal Stevens caught my mom's attention.

"Who does Mr. Goshen send to the principal?"

"Charlie, me, lots of students."

"Charlie, will you be sent to the principal's office again because of Mr. Goshen?"

"I hope not, but maybe."

"We can't have Charlie going to the principal's office." My mom entered my head.

No mind reading at school, but if you need to use your ability to get out of going to the principal's office, I'll allow it. Be very careful, and make sure the principal is nowhere close. I nodded.

Maya looked at me with a crinkled forehead. I shrugged, playing it off like it was nothing, but my mom's concern about the principal was the opposite of nothing. It was freaking me out!

Twelve

On Monday morning, I strapped on my backpack and rode my bike to school. Since I was early to school, the hallways were quiet. I unloaded my backpack in my locker. When I knocked on the door to Mr. Goshen's classroom, nobody responded. I peeked in to see an empty classroom. I glanced both ways in the hallway for a sign of him, but I didn't hear or see anything. It was a ghost town.

I hurried to his desk and searched through the papers on top, looking for anything that could help us prove he wasn't a good teacher. The only thing I found was an envelope with his name and address on it. I scribbled the address into my notebook thinking it might come in handy later.

While I stared at the drawers in his desk, trying to decide if I should open them, I heard footsteps. I circled around to the front of the desk and sat in the closest student's desk.

"Charlie, you are here early," Mr. Goshen asked.

"Can you check over my homework with me?" I asked. "I want to make sure I did it correctly."

"I suppose," he said, walking to me and taking the assignment from me. I followed along as he read my assignment out loud. When he finished, he handed the assignment back to me.

"Good work," he said. "Much better than your previous work."

"Thanks," I said. "Do you mind if I sit in here until the bell rings?"

"As long as you are quiet."

He returned to his desk. I opened my notebook and pretended to read something, but I looked at Mr. Goshen, concentrating on his mind. I entered his thoughts and learned of his teaching plans for the day. He turned his attention to the computer, and it felt like I was reading the websites and articles he visited. All the articles centered around a wrestler named Tommy Thunder. One article talked about how they thought he would lose in his upcoming match. That made Mr. Goshen angry, and I realized what was happening.

"Hot Spaghetti!" I whispered. Mr. Goshen looked at me and I looked down, leaving his thoughts.

"What did you say Charlie?"

"Nothing. Thanks for letting me sit here," I said. I hurried out of the classroom and went to the library. I searched for Tommy Thunder on the internet and learned more about him. He had been wrestling for a few years and risen to the top of the pro-wrestling circuit faster than anyone expected. According to the internet, he gained fans from his fearless attitude. He was wrestling in a match Saturday night, but after that match, he wasn't going to compete again until January for personal reasons.

Finally, I pulled up some pictures of him and examined them. I definitely saw a resemblance between Mr. Goshen and Tommy Thunder. Then I found something that said he grew up in Silver Lake, NY. *Hot diggity dog!*

I closed the computer and went to my locker, looking for Maya. I didn't see her, so I searched the hallways until I found her with Amy and a couple other girls. She spotted me across the hall. I waved her over to me.

"Tommy Thunder is Mr. Goshen," I blurted out.

"Slow down, Charlie." I took a deep breath.

"I think Mr. Goshen is a wrestler named Tommy Thunder and he is wrestling as Tommy on Saturday."

"Are you serious?"

I smiled.

"I also found Mr. Goshen's address," I said.

"What are you thinking?" she asked.

"Field trip after school."

"Where?"

"To his house."

A smile broke out across Maya's face. "I'm in," she said. The bell rang.

"But first, math class," I said.

"And the rest of the school day," she replied.

"Oh, booger, can't we skip school?" I asked.

"Maybe on your planet!" she said. I laughed, and we walked to math class.

Midway through math, a student walked in and handed Mr. Makimoro a pink slip of paper.

"Charlie, the principal would like to see you." I took the slip of paper. There were no notes written about why or when to go. I didn't want to go see the principal, so I pretended like nothing happened.

"Charlie, you should go now," Mr. Makimoro said.

Lickity split. That didn't work. I took my books and left for the office. When I arrived, the secretary smiled and motioned for me to have a seat. My mind was racing the whole time. I didn't know what to say or do, but my parents told me that I had to stay out of his head and keep him out of mine.

Fifteen minutes later, Principal Stevens came out of his office. "Come on in, Charlie," he said. I stood and took a deep breath, and then sat in the chair opposite him behind the big wooden desk.

"How are you adjusting to Silver Lake?" he asked.

Does he know I'm from Europa? Lickity split. Don't think about Europa. Focus.

"I'm doing well," I said.

"I know it can be hard moving to a new school." I nodded. "If you need anything, please don't hesitate to come to me for help."

"Okay."

"Silver Lake is much different from ..." he paused for a moment, and then said "Cleveland" with a grin.

He knows something. Is he one of us? I felt a presence attempting to enter my head, so I channeled all my energy there, stopping whatever he was doing. His smile turned to a frown. He wasn't able to read me.

"Charlie, you can return to class. Mrs. Turner will write you a pass." He smiled again at me. I felt a chill ripple through my body as I rose from my seat and left the office.

With my mind filled with ideas about Principal Stevens and who he might be, my heart started racing, and panic set in. I didn't want to be in school anymore. My walk through the hallways turned into a jog and then a sprint. I ran out the front door of the school.

I grabbed my bike from the rack and pedaled home as fast as I could. I flung open the door and collapsed on the couch, out of breath and energy from keeping Mr. Stevens out of my head and from the sprint home.

"What is it?" my dad asked from the dining room table.

"Principal Stevens." I showed him the memory of our interaction.

"What do you think?"

"I agree that he knows something, but it's hard to say what."

"You haven't learned anything about him yet?"

"Nothing."

"I don't want to go back to that school."

"He could just be a Europan refugee."

"Then why wouldn't he say that?"

"Because he doesn't know who you are either."

"Or he's not from Europa."

"That's not likely," my dad said.

"What do I do?"

"You just have to sit tight."

"Why do I have to wear tights?" I asked.

My dad chuckled. "Sit tight means just wait it out for now, don't do anything or tell anyone,"

"But what does that have to do with tights?"

"I don't know. I just know the saying," my dad said.

"I can't tell Maya still?" I asked.

"No. We don't want to put her in danger somehow. If he's not a refugee, he could be a spy."

"But ..."

"No. Not right now."

"I have to sit back. I can't try to read his mind."

"Let your mother and me take care of that."

"Fine."

Why won't my parents let me do anything? Oh, booger. Being a middle schooler is the worst.

"Can you call the school so I don't get in trouble for leaving?"

"Of course."

"Dad, I'm tired."

"You need to rest. You are pushing yourself too much." He motioned to the couch, so I sprawled across and fell asleep in a few seconds.

Thirteen

When I arrived at school the next day, Maya was waiting at our lockers.

"What happened?"

"Nothing, really. Principal Stevens wanted to make sure I was adjusting here."

"Wait, you didn't get in trouble?"

"Nope."

"You just went to the principal's office to talk."

"He sent for me."

"That's weird."

I didn't know what to say. I couldn't tell her that the principal read my mind or that he might be an alien. I had to lie to her. It didn't feel right.

"Did you look up Tommy Thunder?" I asked to change the subject.

"Yes. It's hard to tell from the pictures for sure, but I think you're right. Tommy Thunder is Mr. Goshen," she asked.

"Do you want to go to his house today after school?"

"I don't know, Charlie. Are you sure about this?"

"Not really, but I think we can get our proof."

"If we get in trouble, my parents will ground me forever. No basketball, no track, nothing."

"We won't get in trouble! We are just knocking on his door. Trust me." I winked at her.

She groaned.

After school, Maya and I walked across town to Mr. Goshen's neighborhood. When we turned on to his street, I was amazed at the size of the house. I didn't know Earthly houses were this big. It looked like a few families could live in each one.

7024 Brandt Street was a mansion. It was three stories with large pillars on the front porch. The driveway circled around the back to a large detached garage.

"Mr. Goshen lives here?" I asked.

"Pro-wrestlers can make a lot of money," Maya said.

"I hope he's home," I said. I took the packet of ketchup in my pocket and smeared it on my arm. "Let's do this." We walked up the driveway and rang the doorknob. I heard footsteps, and a few minutes later Mr. Goshen answered the door.

"Mr. Goshen, I didn't know you lived here," I lied. The words felt dirty coming out of my mouth.

"What's wrong with your arm?"

"I fell and scraped it. Can I use your bathroom to rinse it off? I don't want it to get infected."

"Where are your parents?"

"We are on our way home, and I fell. It will just be a few minutes. I won't make a mess."

"Please, Mr. Goshen," Maya said.

"Fine," he groaned. He opened the door and let us into his large dining room. A large wooden table with eight chairs filled the room and opened into the kitchen. "The bathroom is down the hallway, second door on the right." He pointed forward.

"Thank you." I hurried down the hallway, hoping Maya could keep him occupied for a few minutes. I made it to the second door and opened it to find the bathroom. I scrubbed my arm clean and then peeked out the door. Maya was talking with Mr. Goshen. He was facing the opposite direction. I slid out the door and shut it, then opened the next door.

The room was an office with a desk and computer. The bookcase was filled with trophies. I walked to the trophies and saw Thomas Goshen written on them. They were all wrestling trophies. Posters and pictures of Tommy Thunder were on the shelves and the wall, too.

"What's this?" I picked up an oversized black belt with WWE Champion written in gold letters. I took a picture with the small camera I'd borrowed from my mom. Then I opened the closet and found three of Tommy Thunder's costumes and his mask. *Perfect.* I snapped more pictures and then hurried out of the room. The conversation had stopped. I walked up to them.

"Thanks so much," I said. Mr. Goshen grunted.

Maya and I walked out the door. When we got to the end of the driveway, I showed her the pictures I'd taken. She looked closely at the trophies and plaques, and the posters on the wall, along with the pictures of the costumes.

"Yes, you were right! Mr. Goshen *is* Tommy Thunder!" she said.

"Now we have to figure out how this helps us with his class," I said.

"I think he needs to keep this a secret. It's part of the pro wrestling scene—the secret identity," she said.

"How does that help us?" I asked.

"I don't know yet," she said.

I stayed busy the rest of the week keeping up with our schoolwork and playing basketball. I spent Wednesday and Thursday afternoons practicing at the park. Tryouts were coming up, and I wanted to be ready. It was windy and cold, so Blake and Malik weren't there.

Doubts ran through my head as I practiced. Blake had told me the last time I saw him that I had nothing to worry about. Maybe it was Caden telling me I wouldn't make the team, or Maya's doubts about me that made me unsure, but I kept practicing through the cold. I dribbled and shot the ball until I couldn't feel my hands anymore.

Maya, on the other hand, was worried about English class, not her tryouts. She knew she'd make the basketball team, but on the latest English assignment she'd earned a B. She was disappointed with the grade, but her parents were happy with the improvement. They told her she could try out for basketball. They also said her grade needed to keep improving to stay on the team. She was expected to earn A's in all her classes.

Maya didn't think an A was possible in Mr. Goshen's class. She kept saying we needed a different teacher, but neither of us knew how to get a new teacher, even with the realization that Mr. Goshen was a pro wrestler.

On top of basketball and Mr. Goshen, I received an email Friday morning from the library. Caden hadn't returned *The Giver*. I decided to ask him about the book, even though I was worried it wouldn't end well. I found him wandering the hallways with Jordan before school.

"Hey," I said.

"What do you want?"

"Do you have *The Giver* with you?"

"No."

"Where is it?"

"I think my mom returned it."

"She didn't. It's due tomorrow."

He shrugged.

"What am I supposed to do?"

"Not my problem," he said.

"You are the one who took the book from me."

"What did you say?" Caden said, backing me into a locker.

"Just leave him alone," Jordan said.

"Is there a problem here?" Mr. Goshen asked, coming out of nowhere.

"Nope," Caden said, shoving me into the locker in plain sight of Mr. Goshen. Mr. Goshen pulled Caden away from me.

"Stop causing trouble," Mr. Goshen said.

"I'm sorry," I said even though I didn't really do anything.

"You're okay, Charlie. I was talking to Caden." He turned and stared into Caden's eyes.

"I didn't—" Caden started.

"Enough," Mr. Goshen said. He motioned for Caden, and they walked away. I was stunned.

"Charlie, are you okay?" Amy asked. "I saw Caden push you."

"I'm fine. Mr. Goshen pulled him away before he could hurt me."

"Good," Amy said.

Maya waved from across the hallway and joined us.

"Mr. Goshen just saved me from a possible Caden beat down," I said. "I think that ruins your theory that they are both out to get me, and I still don't have any ideas about the Tommy Thunder thing."

"What are you talking about?" Amy asked.

"Mr. Goshen is a pro-wrestler named Tommy Thunder. Also, he knows Caden somehow outside of school. We are trying to find a way to get him to quit."

Maya stared at me with her eyes open wide and her lips pursed.

"Wait, what?" Amy repeated.

"Mr. Goshen is a pro-wrestler named—"

"She didn't mean repeat the whole thing again," Maya said.

I sensed frustration in her voice.

"What's wrong?" I asked. I think she was mad that I told Amy about Tommy Thunder. Maya didn't say anything.

"Remember when we heard Caden and Mr. Goshen talking about wrestling?" Maya said. I nodded. "What if Caden knows Mr. Goshen is Tommy Thunder? What if that's why Mr. Goshen told him not to worry about his grade?"

"What if what?" I asked.

"Caden is using the Tommy Thunder against him," Amy said.

"Exactly. That's how Caden is getting an A," Maya added.

"Hot booger!" I said.

Maya and Amy turned to me and cracked up.

"I meant to say Hot Spaghetti," I mumbled.

"That's not any better," Amy said. They laughed even harder.

"What do we do now?" I said, trying to curb their laughter.

"We need to confront Mr. Goshen," Amy said.

"Or find proof that Caden is blackmailing him," Maya said.

"So, what do we do now?"

"Halloween is coming up," Maya said.

"Halloween. Right. Wait, what does that have to do with anything?"

Last year, my family and I had been utterly confused when costumed kids came to our door. But now I was one of those kids, and I needed to fit in with the crowd, so I had come up with the perfect costume idea.

"Let's go trick-or-treating to Mr. Goshen's house. Do you have a costume, Charlie?" Maya asked.

"Yes."

"What is it?" Amy asked.

"I'm not telling yet. I don't want to ruin the surprise." I couldn't wait to see Maya's face on Halloween when I showed up in my costume.

"Does your costume come with a mask?" Maya asked.

"Yes."

"And yours, Amy?" she asked. Amy nodded. "Good. That's how we will do it."

"Do what, Maya? I can't read your mind," Amy said. Maya and I chuckled.

"On Halloween, we will trick-or-treat to Mr. Goshen's house in costume."

"And do what?" I asked.

"Get proof that Caden is blackmailing him," Maya said.

"How?" Amy asked.

"I think you might be able to do something that will help us find proof," Maya said to me.

"My parents don't want me to do it right now."

"Do what?" Amy asked.

"It's one time. It will be fine," Maya said, ignoring Amy's comment and my slip.

I sighed. "Maybe," I said.

"What are you two talking about?" Amy said, almost in a shout.

"I'm really good at dancing," I said. Maya burst out laughing. "But my parents won't let me dance."

"Charlie, I can't wait to see you dancing," Maya said, and I couldn't help myself; I started laughing too.

"What?" Amy asked again, but before long the contagious laughter caught her. She cracked up, too. None of us could stop until the bell rang, and at that point, Amy didn't have the chance to ask any more questions.

Lickity split. That was a close one! I can't reveal my secret to anyone else.

Fourteen

Somehow Maya, Amy, and I had to find proof that Caden was blackmailing Mr. Goshen. Maya wanted me to use my ability, but I didn't think that was the right idea.

While I thought about what to do instead, I put the final touches on my Halloween costume. My mom had dyed my costume blue on Friday. Today, we painted the mask blue to match the rest of the costume. When we finished my mask, my mother had to finish my sister Katie's costume. Katie said most of her friends were dressing up as princesses, but she wanted to be a zombie. They finished her costume with a half hour to spare. My sister and I got dressed and ready for our first trick-or-treating experience. My dad was staying home to pass out candy while my mom went with my sister.

"What kind of candy did you get?" I asked my mom. I had heard in school that the type of candy determined whether your house was a good stop. I heard my classmates bragging about the candy at their house.

"I forgot to get some. I'll run to the store," my dad said.

"Trick-or-treating starts in ten minutes. You don't have enough time."

"I'll just be late."

"I don't think you can do that."

"Why not?"

"I think to be a stop, you have to be open with lights on from six to eight or else kids will pass by your house."

"Maybe we have some candy in our house." My dad and I went into the kitchen and looked through the pantry. I didn't see anything that could be passed out in bulk until I looked at the top shelf. The shelf was filled with red boxes of popcorn.

"Do you have the same idea that I do?" I asked.

Yes, he said in my head.

We grabbed all the popcorn boxes off the shelf. "Should we pass it out popped?"

"I don't know," he said.

I looked at the clock. "It will take forever to pop it."

"What if I run out?" he asked.

"I think that's okay. Maya said they ran out of candy last year."

"Perfect."

"Charlie, are you ready to go?" my mom asked.

"Almost." I helped my dad empty all twenty-four boxes of popcorn. With six bags in each box, my dad had enough bags for one hundred and forty-four kids. That had to be enough. I had no idea if popcorn was an acceptable treat to pass out, but if it wasn't, hopefully nobody would know it was my house.

I met my sister and mom in the living room. Mom handed me a canvas bag, and we loaded up in the car.

"I'll pick you up here about eight," my mom said as I shut the car door at Maya's house. I waved as she backed out of the driveway.

I knocked on Maya's door.

"Hello, Ninja," I said. She wore all black with a black hood and a black scarf covering most of her face, except for her eyes. Her skirt and top were outlined in red and she had two swords tucked into a loop on both sides of her.

"Charlie?" she asked.

"Yes.

"You are an alien." She started laughing.

"I am!" She looked from top to bottom at my bright blue costume with the blue mask and big black eyes and tiny nose and mouth. "It's not exactly right, but it's the best I could do."

"Is this what ..." she looked behind her, then continued, "real aliens look like?"

"In a way. I am bright blue with big eyes in my natural body, but that's about it."

"Charlie?" Maya's mom asked, walking up behind her. She wasn't wearing a costume.

"Nope. I am an alien invader," I said. Maya laughed again. Her mom smiled. We heard a knock on the door.

"Trick-or-treat!" Amy said. "Or smell my feet." Her outfit was like Maya's except her ninja costume was red.

"Smell your feet? Okay, if you want me to." I started to bend over. Maya and Amy started laughing.

"Ewww. It's a saying," Amy said. "I didn't mean it."

"Hot Spaghetti, that's a weird saying!"

"And Hot Spaghetti isn't?" Amy asked with a giggle.

"Good point!"

"C'mon, let's get going," Maya said. "I want to fill my bag before we go to Mr. Goshen's house. 'Bye, Mom!"

"Call us if you need picked up or need anything. Be safe," Mrs. Bennett said.

"'Bye, Mrs. Bennett."

Maya lived at the top of the street, so we went next door and continued down the street to the cul-de-sac. At every door, we all shouted "Trick-or-treat!" An adult would put a piece or two of candy in our bag, and on to the next house we'd go. Maya and Amy were fast so I had to jog most of the time to keep up. Halfway down her street, we slowed down a bit.

"Lickity split, I need a break. This trick-or-treating is hard work," I said.

"What time is it?" she asked.

I looked at my watch. "6:17."

We approached the next house. The lights were off and it was dark, but I heard ominous music playing from somewhere.

"Shouldn't we pass this one?"

"Nope," Maya said, but she slowed her, letting me take the lead. Amy trailed behind. I followed the path around to the door, but I felt someone else nearby. I looked around, but I didn't see anyone.

"Maya, somebody is here," I whispered. She didn't say anything.

"Happy Halloween!" shouted a gorilla who jumped in our path.

"Hot diggity dog!" I yelled, and shuddered. Maya and Amy cracked up.

"That was a good one, Jerry," Maya said. The gorilla gave her a high five. Then he grabbed a bowl from behind a tree and placed two giant candy bars in our bags.

"Thanks," I mumbled, and we left the house.

"You knew that was going to happen!" I said.

"Yes. I thought with your ability, it might not work. But it did, and it was great," Maya said.

"Wait, what ability?" Amy asked.

Lickity split. "I have really good vision," I said. "I knew he was there." Amy looked at me funny, but didn't say anything about my "vision ability."

"Come on, no you didn't," Maya said.

We finished up the last few houses on her street and turned toward Mr. Goshen's neighborhood.

"Do you have any ideas of how to find proof about Caden?" I asked Maya and Amy.

"I was hoping you had an idea," Maya said. She nudged me in my arm.

"What was that for?" I asked. She sighed.

"Try asking about Tommy Thunder?" Amy said. "If that doesn't work, ask about Caden. Maybe he will slip and tell us something we don't know."

Maya nodded and nudged me again. Amy walked out ahead.

"Use your ability to find proof," Maya whispered.

"My parents don't want me to use my ability right now," I muttered back.

"Please, Charlie," she said.

I let out a deep breath.

"Maybe."

Fifteen

"Wow," I said. Mr. Goshen's street was filled with kids in all sorts of costumes. I saw princesses, ghosts, pumpkins, and even forks.

"Lots of kids come to this neighborhood because the houses give out king-size candy bars," Maya said.

"King-size? Does that mean they are the size of a bed?"

"Hanging out with you is never boring," she said laughing. "No, they are bigger than the normal size, but not that big!"

"Oh."

We walked to Mr. Goshen's house. The porch light was on, and a few kids were at the door. Mr. Goshen handed out a few small pieces of candy.

"Those are not king-size," I said.

"Of course, he wouldn't give out good candy," Amy said. She looked down the street. "Most of the kids are past his house. This is probably a good time."

"Let's do it." We picked up our pace, crossed the street, and hurried up the driveway. Before we rang the doorbell, I asked one more time. "Are you ready?"

Maya and Amy nodded. I rang the doorbell. Mr. Goshen answered with a bowl of candy with Tootsie Rolls and Dum Dums, the bottom barrel of Halloween candy.

"Mr. Goshen, we know your secret," I said.

"What secret?"

"That you are Tommy Thunder,"

"Seriously?" he said.

"Yes," I said. Amy and Maya nodded.

"That's ridiculous," Mr. Goshen said. Maya shoved her phone in his face and scrolled through the pictures of his wrestling gear. I concentrated in on his mind. He was surprised but not worried. He didn't care about us knowing he was Tommy Thunder, and I didn't know what to do next.

"How come Caden is the only one getting an A in your class?" Maya asked.

"He earned it."

"Yeah, right. He's blackmailing you," Amy said.

Mr. Goshen laughed.

"He is working hard. I suggest you three do the same. Now leave my house." Maya pushed me forward into the doorway. She wanted me to use my ability.

"C'mon, do it," she whispered.

"How is Caden getting an A?" I asked.

"I already told you that he is working hard," Mr. Goshen said. He began to shut the door, so I held the door open with my hand to see if my question worked. I focused on him and saw an image of Caden with Mr. Goshen. They were in Mr. Goshen's classroom. Caden was asking him about *The Giver* assignment, and Mr. Goshen was giving him some pointers of how to do the assignment. Then another memory appeared in my mind. He was Caden's football coach a few years ago. After the game, a man yelled and shoved Caden. I felt Mr. Goshen's disgust at that man as he consoled Caden. *I shouldn't have seen that.* I started to leave his mind when a sad memory entered his head. I felt his pain, but I didn't want to know why.

This isn't right. I need to get out of his head.

"Get out of who's head?" Mr. Goshen said.

Lickity split! I talked to him telepathically by accident. *This isn't good.*

"What isn't good?" Mr. Goshen asked, confused.

"What are you talking about, Mr. Goshen?" Amy asked.

"We need to go," I said to Amy and Maya. "Before he realizes what just happened."

I shut the door on Mr. Goshen and hurried down the driveway. Amy and Maya trailed behind me. When we reached the sidewalk, I stopped to catch my breath for a second.

"What happened?" Maya asked. We took a few more steps down the sidewalk, away from Mr. Goshen's house.

"Yeah, I'm totally confused," Amy added.

"Caden isn't blackmailing Mr. Goshen, and then I saw something that I shouldn't," I said. "I couldn't do it anymore." A wave of fatigue was coming over me. I stopped and sat on the ground.

"Do what?" Amy asked.

"I need a break," I said. "I'm tired."

"Charlie?" Maya said, again, and again. But her voice was fading, and I couldn't keep my eyes open any more.

Sixteen

"Charlie, wake up, man." I opened my eyes to see Blake staring at me. Malik and Amy were next to him. Maya stood behind them on the phone.

"Hey," I croaked out.

"Are you all right?"

"I'll be okay," I said. Blake lent me a hand so I could sit up. We were hidden a bit between two trees in someone's yard. "Where did you come from?"

"Right place at the right time. We were trick-or-treating at this house when we saw you fall. We ran over to help and saw that it was you. What happened?"

"Hard to explain. Sometimes I overwork myself." They looked at each other.

"My mom is on her way," Maya said. "Are you okay?"

"I'll be fine," I said.

"Maya, Amy, this is Blake and Malik."

"This is Maya?" Blake said. He smiled and winked at me.

"Is there something wrong with your eye?" I asked Blake.

"Charlie, you are clueless," Blake said. Amy and Maya whispered something to each other.

"Wait, Charlie, you play basketball with these guys?" Maya asked.

"Yeah."

"Huh. Maybe you will make the team then," Maya said.

"He will," Blake said. "But we will beat you when we play."

"We have to play each other?"

"Yeah, man, and Silver Lake always loses to Adams in basketball."

"Oh, booger."

Amy, Maya, Blake, and Malik shook their heads and laughed.

A car pulled up to us. Maya's mom rolled down the window.

"It looks like you are feeling better," Maya's mom said to me. "You had us worried. Come on, I'm taking you home. I already talked to your dad. He said sometimes you exert yourself a little too much without realizing it."

"See you around," I said to Blake and Malik.

"Good luck at the tryouts," Malik said.

I waved and got into the back seat of the car with Amy. Maya sat in the font.

"I'm sorry, Mrs. Bennett." I said, embarrassed. "I don't know what happened."

"It's okay, Charlie. I'm glad you are okay." She drove us a few minutes away to my street. When she parked in my driveway, my dad came out the front door to meet me and help me out of the car.

"Thank you so much, Mrs. Bennett. We will make sure he gets some rest."

"I'll be fine," I said. I managed a wave, and with my dad's help, I made it through the front door and on to the couch.

"Lucky for you, I have some popcorn left," he said with a smile. He stuck a bag in the microwave and brought me a glass of water. "Mom and Katie are still trick-or-treating. What happened? Tell me everything." I told him about trick-or-treating and then going to Mr. Goshen's house. I told him about speaking to him through his head by accident. He didn't look happy.

"I knew right away it was wrong when I saw a memory of Caden and Mr. Goshen. It was much different than any other mind reading I've done. It was so personal."

"Yes, son. What did you see?"

"Just a sad memory, but it felt wrong for me to know it because they didn't tell me the story."

"Exactly, Charlie. I think you understand now why we can't use our ability everywhere on Earth."

"I'm sorry, Dad." I felt him enter my head. For me, that was normal, that was okay. We told each other everything because we were family. It wasn't okay when I didn't have permission to be in someone's head or memories.

"What do I do now?" I asked my dad.

"About what?"

"Maya and Mr. Goshen. She has to get a better grade."

"It sounds like you two have to work harder. Have you asked Mr. Goshen for help?"

"Sort of."

"That's where you need to start."

"Right."

"Charlie, life on Earth is different, but some things are universal. Hard work equals success."

"What if Mr. Goshen knows that it was us at his house? What if he knows I was in his head?"

"You told me that Maya wouldn't tell anyone about us because nobody would believe her. I think the same will be true here. Don't worry about it, Charlie. Mr. Goshen is going to doubt himself if he has any recollection of what happened."

The doorbell rang. My dad motioned to the door. I hurried and answered the door.

"Trick-or-treat!" shouted two super heroes. I gave them each a bag of popcorn.

"Popcorn? That's not candy."

"Nope, it's better than candy," I said.

"No, it's not," one of them said. "I'd rather have a Tootsie Roll than popcorn." He put the popcorn in his bag and walked away. I shut the door.

"Have any kids liked the popcorn?" I asked.

"A few here and there, but it's fine. Charlie, do you feel okay?"

"Tired, but okay."

"Good, but there's a reason we tell you to take it slow. There's a reason you have to train with us. Charlie, tonight could have been much worse." I felt the weight of his words.

"I won't do that again."

The door opened. My mother and Katie walked into the house.

"How was your night?" my mom asked.

"It was ... crazy." My mom looked to my dad. I knew they were having a conversation, but I didn't need to be a part of it. I turned to Katie.

"Let me see what you got." I opened her bag and searched it. "Nothing good!"

"You only like popcorn," Katie said.

"True. So, what now?"

"How about a scary movie?" my mom said.

"Sounds great," my dad said.

Seventeen

Monday morning, I received an email from the library. I took a deep breath and opened it. *The Giver* had been returned! I ran down the stairs.

"Caden returned the book! I'm not going to jail!" My family looked up from their breakfasts, and we all laughed. I finished getting ready and headed to school, nervous about what I had to do.

I met Maya at our lockers. We had messaged back and forth on Sunday, so she knew a little more about what had happened on Halloween.

"Hey," I said. "Is Amy coming too?"

"No," she said. "I think she's a little freaked out about what happened."

"What do you mean?"

"You passed out and said some weird things. I told her you had a rare brain condition, but that didn't make her feel any better."

"What should I do?"

"I don't know, Charlie. You can't tell her the truth. I guess you need to be more careful about what you say and do around her."

"Great. Be careful. Why does everyone tell me that?"

Maya shrugged. I felt a lump form in my throat as we walked to Mr. Goshen's classroom. My dad told me not to worry, but I couldn't help it. The door was open, but both of us paused before walking into the room. I saw him sitting at his desk.

"Here goes nothing," I said. I walked in and Maya followed me to his desk. "Mr. Goshen, can you help us with this assignment? I know it's not due until Wednesday, but we want to do well on it."

"I can't do it for you, but if you have some specific questions, I can answer those." He motioned to the table at the front of the room. We sat in the empty chairs and he pulled up his chair.

"I'm confused about dependent clauses," I said.

"And we both aren't sure how to support our responses with quotes from the book," Maya added.

"I can help you with both of those questions. Let's start with Charlie's question first."

Maya and I spent the next fifteen minutes with Mr. Goshen and left feeling much more confident of our ability to do well in his class. He still wasn't the friendliest teacher, but I guess that didn't matter if we were learning.

"Do you really think Caden earned his A?" Maya asked on our way to our lockers.

"Yes. I saw a memory of him asking for help from Mr. Goshen. Mr. Goshen was Caden's football coach a few years ago."

"So Caden wasn't afraid to ask him for help," Maya said.

"Yeah, and guess what? Caden returned my book to the library," I told Maya. "Maybe he doesn't hate me after all."

"He hasn't done anything really mean to you lately."

"Except when he shoved me in the corn maze."

"What? I didn't know that happened."

"I forgot you didn't know that. I don't know. Maybe it's not his fault he's a bully."

"What do you mean?"

"I saw something else in Mr. Goshen's head. I don't think we know the whole story about Caden."

"Oh," Maya said.

Amy walked over, interrupting our conversation.

"Are you talking about spaghetti or boogers again, Charlie?" Amy asked. I chuckled.

"Are you feeling better?" she asked.

"Oh, I'm fine," I said with a smile.

"Are you sure? I was ..." She looked to the floor, and I could tell she was going to say scared or worried.

"Seriously, I'm fine," I said.

"Maya told me about your condition. Does that happen a lot?"

"Nope. Hopefully never again."

"Good," she said. "Did you hear about the house that handed out popcorn bags on Halloween?" Amy asked.

"Where was that?" I asked.

"Hunter Woods?" she said.

"Don't you live on Hunter Woods?" Maya asked me.

I shook my head no. She got the hint.

The bell rang.

"See you guys later," Amy said. Maya and I walked to math class.

"That was your house, wasn't it?" Maya asked.

"Yep. We forgot to get candy, and that is all we had."

"You had enough popcorn to hand out to all the trick-or-treaters?"

"We like popcorn a lot."

"Popped or unpopped?"

"Unpopped."

"Your family is hopeless!" We laughed and took our seats, ready for another day at Silver Lake Middle School.

I was the alien in the room, but I didn't feel like an outcast anymore. The announcements came on and I listened to the lunch menu and events happening for the week. I'd almost forgotten! Basketball tryouts were in two days! My heart beat faster with excitement about playing basketball. Then Principal Stevens started talking, and all the excitement I felt vanished. I needed to figure out who he was. It couldn't wait any longer.

ALIEN KID

AFTERWORD

Thank you for reading Alien Kid 2. Please leave a review online. Reviews are very important to authors and help readers discover new books.

If you loved this book, then you will want to read Maya's Diary that tells her side of the story as she meets Charlie and learns he is an alien. Maya's Diary is free to my email list so sign up at kristenotte.com.

I'm excited about this series, so I hope you will follow along with Charlie's journey on Earth. Book three is in the works!

Thank you to my editor, Candace Johnson, for always fitting me into her schedule. Thanks to Glendon Haddix for his amazing cover design.

Thanks to my family and friends for not thinking I am crazy for writing kids' books about pugs and aliens.

Thanks to Lincoln for sleeping so I have time to write!

Brian, I couldn't do this without your support. I love you.

John 14:12

ABOUT THE AUTHOR

Author Kristen Otte writes books for children, teens, and adults. She loves writing books that make kids laugh. Most of the time Kristen is chasing someone around her house–her son, her dogs, even her husband. If she isn't doing that, she is probably writing, reading, or enjoying the outdoors.

BOOKS BY KRISTEN OTTE

The Adventures of Zelda: A Pug Tale
The Adventures of Zelda: The Second Saga
The Adventures of Zelda: Pug and Peach
The Adventures of Zelda: The Four Seasons
The Adventures of Zelda: The One & Only Pug
The Perfect Smile (Eastbrook 0.5)
The Photograph (Eastbrook 1)
The Evolution of Lillie Gable (Eastbrook 2)
Alien Kid
Alien Kid 2

www.kristenotte.com.

Made in the USA
Columbia, SC
13 September 2017